*continued . . .*

# THE
# UNNATURAL
# INQUIRER

## SIMON R. GREEN

**ACE BOOKS, NEW YORK**

**THE BERKLEY PUBLISHING GROUP**
**Published by the Penguin Group**
**Penguin Group (USA) Inc.**
**375 Hudson Street, New York, New York 10014, USA**
Penguin Group (Canada), 90 Eglinton Avenue East, Suite 700, Toronto, Ontario M4P 2Y3, Canada
(a division of Pearson Penguin Canada Inc.)
Penguin Books Ltd., 80 Strand, London WC2R 0RL, England
Penguin Group Ireland, 25 St. Stephen's Green, Dublin 2, Ireland (a division of Penguin Books Ltd.)
Penguin Group (Australia), 250 Camberwell Road, Camberwell, Victoria 3124, Australia
(a division of Pearson Australia Group Pty. Ltd.)
Penguin Books India Pvt. Ltd., 11 Community Centre, Panchsheel Park, New Delhi—110 017, India
Penguin Group (NZ), 67 Apollo Drive, Rosedale, North Shore 0632, New Zealand
(a division of Pearson New Zealand Ltd.)
Penguin Books (South Africa) (Pty.) Ltd., 24 Sturdee Avenue, Rosebank, Johannesburg 2196,
South Africa

Penguin Books Ltd., Registered Offices: 80 Strand, London WC2R 0RL, England

THE UNNATURAL INQUIRER

An Ace Book / published by arrangement with the author

PRINTING HISTORY
Ace hardcover edition / January 2008
Ace mass-market edition / January 2009

Copyright © 2008 by Simon R. Green.
Excerpt from *Just Another Judgement Day* copyright © 2009 by Simon R. Green.
Cover art by Jonathan Barkat.
Cover design by Judith Lagerman.

ISBN: 978-0-441-01667-9

ACE
Ace Books are published by The Berkley Publishing Group,
a division of Penguin Group (USA) Inc.,
375 Hudson Street, New York, New York 10014.
ACE and the "A" design are trademarks belonging to Penguin Group (USA) Inc.

PRINTED IN THE UNITED STATES OF AMERICA

10  9  8  7  6  5  4  3  2  1

In the Nightside, the night never ends. Hidden away in the dark, magical heart of London, dreams go walking in borrowed flesh, and temptation and salvation are always on sale. You can find anything you want in the Nightside; if it doesn't find you first.

Hot neon, dark shadows, more sin than you can shake a credit card at, wild clubs, and madder music. Put on your dancing shoes, and dance till you bleed. The night goes on and on, and the fun never stops. And someone, somewhere, has a bullet with your name on it.

My name is John Taylor. Private eye, lost soul, looking for salvation in the damnedest places. I have a special gift for finding things, but mostly what I find is trouble. Hire me if you want to know the truth. I can't guarantee to deliver justice, or even a happy ending . . . but when the bodies have stopped dropping and all the comforting illusions have been ripped away, at least you'll have the truth to hug to your bruised heart.

I'm John Taylor, and this is the Nightside; and this is not a story for anyone who believes everything he reads in the papers.

# ONE

*The Wrath of the Loa*

One of the many problems with working as a private eye, not counting all the many people who want to kill you, often for perfectly good reasons, is that you have to wait for the work to come to you. And since I refuse to sit around my office, on the grounds that all the high tech my secretary, Cathy, has installed intimidates the hell out of me, I seem to spend most of my time sitting around in bars, waiting for something to happen. Not a bad way to spend your life, all told. But in the end, cases are a lot like buses; you wait around for ages, then three come along at once.

I'm a private eye of the old school, right down to the long white trench coat, the less-than-traditional good looks, and the roguish air of mystery that I go to great lengths to maintain. Always keep them guessing. A good, or more properly bad, reputation can protect you from more things than a Kevlar jump-suit. I investigate cases of the weird and uncanny, the sins and problems too dark and too nasty even for the Nightside. I don't do divorce work, and I don't carry a gun. I've never felt the need.

I'd just finished a fairly straightforward case, when trouble came looking for me. I'd been called in by the slightly hysterical manager of one of the Nightside's most prominent libraries, the H P Lovecraft Memorial Library. Their proud boast: more forbidden tomes under one roof than anywhere else. I'd leafed through some of their proud exhibits in the past and hadn't been impressed. Of course they had the *Necronomicon*, in forty-eight languages, including Braille, and one of the few unexpurgated texts of *The Gospel According to Pontius Pilate*. They even had *Satan's Last Testament*, originally tattooed on the inside of the womb of the Fallen Nun of Lourdes. But a lot of it was strictly tourist stuff. *The Book of Unpronounceable Cults*, *Satanism for Dummies*, and *Coarse Fishing on the River Styx*. Nothing there to expand your mind or endanger your soul.

I'd been called in because twenty-seven of the Library's patrons had been discovered wandering through the stacks wide-eyed and mind-wiped. Not a trace of personality or conscious thought left in them. Which was unusually high for a Monday morning, even in the H P Lovecraft Memorial Library. Using my gift, it didn't take me long to discover that a recently acquired treatise had been reading people . . . I persuaded the book to put the minds back, mostly in the right bodies, and introduced it to the wonders of the Internet. Which should keep it occupied until the Library could send it somewhere else.

So, happy smiles all round, a wallet full of cash (I don't take cheques or plastic, don't ask for credit, as a refusal might involve a back elbow between the eyes), and all in all I was feeling quite pleased with myself . . . until I left the Library and looked down the steps to find Walker and Suzie Shooter waiting for me at the bottom. Probably two of the most dangerous people in the Nightside.

Suzie Shooter, also known as Shotgun Suzie, and *Oh Christ It's Her Run*, is the Nightside's leading bounty hunter. Have shotgun and grenades, will travel. A tall blonde Valkyrie in black motor-cycle leathers, with two bandoliers of bullets criss-crossing over her ample bosom, steel-toed boots, and the coldest gaze in the world. The whole left side of her face was covered in ridged scar tissue, sealing shut one eye and twisting up one side of her mouth in a constant caustic smile. She could have had it fixed easily, but she chose not to. She said it was good for business. It did give her a grim, wounded glamour.

Suzie and I are an item. Safe to say neither of us saw that one coming. We love each other, as best we can.

Walker is even more dangerous to be around, though in more subtle and indirect ways. He looks very much like your average city gent; pin-striped suit, bowler hat, calm air of authority. Someone in the City, you might think, or perhaps a Permanent Under-Secretary to some Minister you never heard of. But Walker polices the Nightside, inasmuch as anyone does, or can. In a place where everything is permitted, and sin and temptation are the order of every day, there are still lines that must not be crossed. For those who do, Walker is waiting.

He used to represent the Authorities, those grey faceless men who owned everything that mattered and took a profit from every dirty and dangerous transaction in the Nightside. Walker spoke in their name, with the Voice they gave him that could not be disobeyed, and he could call in the Army or the Church to back him up, as necessary. But since all the Authorities were killed and eaten during the Lilith War, lots of people had been wondering just where Walker drew his authority from these days. He still had his Voice, and his backup, so everyone went along.

But an awful lot of people were waiting for the other shoe to drop.

He smiled and nodded at me politely, but I ignored him on principle and gave my full attention to Suzie.

"Hello, sweetie. I haven't seen you for a few days."

"I've been working," she said, in her cold, steady voice. "Chasing down a bounty."

"For Walker?" I said, raising an eyebrow.

She shrugged easily, the butt of the shotgun holstered on her back rising briefly behind her head. "His money is as good as anyone else's. And you know I need to keep busy. I only really feel alive when it's death or glory time. You finished with your case?"

"Yes," I said, glancing reluctantly at Walker.

"Then walk with me, John," he said. "I could use your assistance on a rather urgent case."

I went down the steps to join him, taking my time. I'd worked with Walker before, on occasion, though rarely happily. He paid well enough, but he only ever used me for those cases where he didn't want to risk his own people. The kind of cases where he needed someone potentially deniable and utterly expendable. We strode together through the Nightside, Walker on my left and Suzie on my right, and everyone else made sure to give us plenty of room.

"I hired Suzie because someone big and important had gone missing," Walker said easily. "And I needed him found, fast. Nothing unusual there. But unfortunately, Suzie has proven entirely unable to locate the target."

"Not my fault," Suzie said immediately. "I've been through all my usual contacts, and none of them could tell me anything. Even after all the usual bribes and beatings. The man's just vanished. Jumped into a deep hole and pulled it in after him. I'm not even sure he's still in the Nightside."

"Oh, he's still here," said Walker. "I'd know if he'd left."

"Who exactly are we talking about?" I said.

"Max Maxwell," said Walker. "Ah; I take it from your expression that you have at least heard of him."

7

"Who hasn't?" I said. "Max Maxwell; so big they named him twice. Night-club owner, gang boss, fence, and fixer. Also known as the Voodoo Apostate, though I couldn't tell you why."

"The very man," said Walker. "A well-established, very well-connected individual. He tried to have me killed twice, but I'm not one to bear grudges. Anyway, it would appear dear Max came into possession of something rather special, something he should have had more sense than to get involved with. To be exact, the Aquarius Key."

"I know the name," I said, frowning. "Some artifact from the sixties, isn't it? Back when every Major Player had to have their very own Object of Power to be taken seriously. I've never trusted the things. You can never tell when the cosmic batteries are suddenly going to run out of juice, and you're left standing there with a silly-looking lump of art deco in your hand."

"Quite," said Walker. "Still, a very useful tool, the Aquarius Key. Part scientific, part magical, it was created to open and close dimensional doors. This was after the Babalon Working fiasco, you understand."

"Why . . . Aquarius?" I said.

Walker shrugged. "It was the Age. Word is, the Collector had it for a time, which was how he was able to start his marvellous collection of rare and fashionable items. Then he lost it in a card game to old blind Pew, and after that the Key went wandering through many hands, causing mischief and mayhem as it went, until finally it ended up in the possession of Max Maxwell. Where it apparently gave him ideas above his station."

"And that's how he became the Voodoo Apostate?" I said.

"Unfortunately, yes," said Walker. "Voodoo is, first and foremost, a religion in its own right. Its followers worship a wide pantheon of gods, or loas: Papa Legba, Baron Samedi, Erzulie, and Damballa. These personages can be summoned, or invited, into our world, where they possess willing worshippers. Max made himself Apostate by using the power of the Key to drag the loa into this world, whether they wanted to come or not, then thrust them into his own people. Who could then be commanded to serve him in all kinds of useful ways. Inhumanly strong, utterly unfeeling, and almost impossible to kill, they made formidable shock troops."

I winced. "Messing with gods. Always a bad idea."

"Always," said Walker. "Max used his new shock troops to enlarge his territory, with much slaughter and terror; which brought him to my attention. Inevitably, Max became greedy and overstretched himself, spread his control too thin; and the loa broke loose. Max didn't wait for them to come looking for him. He went on the run, taking the Key with him, and none of my people have been able to find him. So I turned to Suzie, with her excellent reputation for finding people who don't want to be found."

Suzie growled something indistinct. I wouldn't want

to be Max Maxwell when she finally got to him. She took a target's attempts to escape capture as a personal insult.

"What makes this case so urgent that you need me?" I said. "Suzie will find him. Eventually."

"The loa have come to the Nightside," said Walker. "And they are not in a good mood. They have possessed a whole crowd of the very best bounty hunters and are currently rampaging through the Nightside, on the trail of Max Maxwell."

"Let them have him," I said. "The man is scum. A jumped-up leg-breaker, who used his voodoo to run protection rackets. Pay up, or he'd turn you into a zombie. You, or someone in your family. Nasty man. Let the loa tear him apart. The Nightside will smell better when he's gone."

"Right," said Suzie. "Wait a minute; if the loa have been possessing all the best bounty hunters . . . why didn't they choose me? I'm the best there is, and I'll shoot the kneecaps off anyone who says otherwise. Why didn't the loa come after me?"

"They wouldn't dare," I said, gallantly.

"Well, there is that, yes," said Suzie. "And unlike some, I'm always careful to keep my protections up to date. A girl can't be too careful."

I pitied anyone or anything dumb enough to dive into Suzie's steel-trap mind, but I wasn't dumb enough to say so out loud. Besides, a new idea had just occurred to me. I looked at Walker.

"Max still has the Aquarius Key. And you want me to get it back for you."

"I knew you'd get there eventually," said Walker. "I want you to find Max and take the Key away from him. Then bring it back to me, so I can stow it away somewhere safe and see Max locked safely away in Shadow Deep."

I would have shuddered, but it was never wise to show weakness in front of Walker. Shadow Deep is the worst prison in the world, carved out of the bedrock deep under the Nightside. It's where we put the really bad ones; or at least the ones we can't just execute and be done with, for one reason or another. Forever dark, never a glimmer of light, once they've sealed you up in your cell, you never leave again. You stay there in your cell, till the day you die. However long it takes.

"Might be kinder to just let the loa have him," I said. "We could always take the Key off whatever's left of his body afterwards."

"No," Walker said immediately. "Partly because the loa will cause havoc looking for him. Like most gods, they can be very single-minded when it comes to revenge. It's already become clear they aren't following standard bounty hunter etiquette and allowing informers to live after they've informed. But mostly I want Max back in my hands because the Nightside takes care of its own problems. Can't let outsiders think they can just walk in here and throw their weight around."

He stopped abruptly, and Suzie and I stopped with

him. He took an old-fashioned gold repeater watch from his waistcoat-pocket, checked the time, put it away, and gave me a measuring look.

"Don't screw this up, John. I'm under a lot of pressure to get this done quickly, efficiently, and with no loose ends. That's why I'm handing this case over to you instead of just flooding the Nightside with my own people. If you can't locate Max, and the Key, within the next three hours, I'll have no choice but to unleash my dogs of war, which will make me very unpopular in all sorts of areas. So don't let me down, John, or I shall be sure to blame it all on you."

Suzie looked at him steadily, and give the man credit, Walker didn't flinch.

"You come for him," Suzie said coldly, "you come for me."

"Sooner or later, I come for everyone," said Walker.

"Under pressure?" I said thoughtfully, and he looked back at me. I grinned right into his calm, collected face. "From whom, precisely? Whom do you serve, now the Authorities are all dead and gone?"

But he just smiled briefly, nodded to me, and tipped his bowler hat to Suzie, then turned and walked away, disappearing unhurriedly back into the night.


Suzie Shooter and I went to the Spider's Web. A sort of up-market cocktail bar, owned by Max Maxwell ever since he had its previous owner killed, stuffed, mounted, and put on display; it was widely known as his seat of power, where he did business with the poor unfortunates who came before him. By the time we got there, the place had already been very thoroughly trashed. Bits of it were still smouldering. Suzie drew her pump-action shotgun from its rear holster with one easy movement and led the way as we entered through the kicked-in front door.

The lobby was wrecked, with bodies everywhere. None of them had died easily. Blood had soaked into the carpet, splashed up the walls, and even stained the ceiling. Severed hands had been piled up in one corner, and all the heads were missing their faces. Suzie and I moved slowly and cautiously between the bodies, but nothing moved. The furniture looked like it had exploded.

Max Maxwell's inner office at the back of the club didn't look much better. No blood or bodies, though, which suggested Max had got out in time. A pack of tarot cards had been left scattered across the top of a huge mahogany desk, which had been cracked casually in half. Thick mats of ivy crawled across all four walls, reportedly part of Max's early-warning system; but every bit of it was dead, withered away as though blasted by a terrible frost. Here and there, something had gouged deep claw-marks through the ivy and into the wood beneath. The bare floor was covered with cabalistic symbols, a whole series of overlapping defence systems.

A lot of good they'd done.

"This man had to be seriously worried to have so many protections in one place," said Suzie.

"He had good reason," I said. "Gods really don't like it when worshippers start forgetting their place and flexing their muscles."

I fired up my gift, and the world changed around me. I couldn't use my gift to pin down Max's current location; I need a specific question to get a specific answer. But there's more than one way to find someone who doesn't want to be found. I opened up my inner eye, my third eye, and Saw the world as it really is. There's a lot going on around us that most people aren't aware of, and it's probably just as well. If they knew who and what we share this world with, an awful lot of them would probably rip their own heads off rather than see it.

There were things in the office with us, drifting on currents unknown to mortal men, filling the aether like the tiny creatures that swarm and multiply in a drop of water. And just as ugly. I focused my gift, concentrating on Max Maxwell, and his ghost image appeared before me—his past, imprinted on Time.

Max was just as big as everyone said he was. A giant of a man, huge and looming even in this semi-transparent state. Eight feet tall, and impressively broad across the chest and shoulders, he wore an impeccably cut cream-coloured suit, presumably chosen to contrast with the deep black of his harsh, craggy face. He looked like he'd been carved out of stone, a great brooding gargoyle in a Saville Row suit. He was scowling fiercely, his huge dark hands clenched into fists.

He stamped silently around his office, as though looking for something. He didn't seem scared, or even concerned. Simply angry. He unlocked a drawer in his desk and brought out something wrapped in a blood-red cloth. He made a series of signs over the bundle and then unwrapped it, revealing a bulky square contraption made up of dully shining metal pieces joined together in a way that made my eyes hurt to look at it. The Aquarius Key, presumably. It looked like a prototype, something that hadn't had all the bugs hammered out of it yet.

Max weighed the thing thoughtfully in one oversized hand, then looked round sharply, as though he'd heard something he didn't like. He gestured grandly with his free hand, and all the cabalistic signs on the floor burst into light. The ivy on the walls writhed and twisted, as though in pain. One by one, the lines on the floor began to gutter and go out. Max headed for the door.

I went after him, Suzie right there at my side. She couldn't see what I was Seeing, but she trusted me.

In as much as she trusted anyone.


We tracked Max Maxwell's ghost half-way across the Nightside. I had to fight to concentrate on his past image. When my inner eye is cranked all the way open, I can See all there is to See in the Nightside, and a lot of it the human mind just isn't equipped to deal with. The endlessly full moon hung low in the star-speckled sky, twenty times the size it should have been. Something with vast membranous wings sailed across the face of the moon, almost eclipsing it. The buildings around us blazed with protective signs, magical defences, and shaped curses scrawled across the storefronts like so much spitting and crackling graffiti. A thousand other ghosts stamped and raged and howled silently all around me, memories trapped in repeating loops of Time, like insects in amber.

Dimensional travellers flashed and flared in and out of existence, just passing through on their way to somewhere more interesting. Demons rode the backs of unsuspecting souls, their claws dug deep into back and shoulder muscles, whispering in their host's ear. You could always tell which ones had been listening; their demons were particularly fat and bloated. Wee winged sprites, pulsing with light, shot up and down the street, fierce as fireworks, buzzing around and above each other in intricate patterns too complex for human eyes. And the Awful Ones, huge and ancient, moved through our streets and buildings as though they weren't even there, about their unguessable business.

I kept my head down, focused on Max Maxwell, and Suzie saw to it that no-one bothered me or got in our way. She had her shotgun out and at the ready, and no-one ever doubted that she'd use it. Suzie had always been a great believer in the scorched-earth solution for all problems, great and small.

Max led us right through the centre of the Nightside, and out the other side, and I had a bad feeling I knew where he was headed. Bad as the Nightside undoubtedly is, even it has its recognised Bad Places, places you simply don't go if you've got any sense. One of these is Fun Faire. It was supposed to be the Nightside's very first amusement park, for adults. Someone's Big Idea; but it never caught on. The people who come to the Nightside aren't interested in artificial thrills; not when there are so many of the real thing available on every street corner. Fun Faire was shut down years ago, and the only reason it's still taking up valuable space is because the various creditors are still arguing over who owns what. Now, it's just a collection of huge rusting rides, great hulking structures left to rot in the cold, uncaring night.

Last I'd heard, they'd run through fourteen major league exorcists, merely trying to keep the place quiet.

Max had chosen Fun Faire as his bolt-hole precisely because so many bad things had happened there. So much death and suffering, so much cheerful slaughter and infernal malice, had turned the Fun Faire grounds into one big psychic null spot. The genius loci had become so awful, so soaked in blood and terror, that no-one could See into it. Which made it a really good place to hide out, for as long as you could stand it.

Suzie and I stopped at the amusement park entrance, and stood there, looking in. Max's ghost image had snapped off the moment he walked through the main archway. I shut down my Sight. The great multi-coloured arch loomed above us, paint peeling and speckled with rust. The old neon letters along the top that had once blazed the words FUN FAIRE! to an unsuspecting public were now cracked and dusty and lifeless. Someone had spray-painted over them ABANDON HOPE ALL YE WHO ENTER HERE. Graveyard humour, but I had to admire their nerve. Beyond the archway it was all dark shapes and darker shadows, the metal bones of old rides standing out in stark silhouettes against the night sky. No lights, anywhere in Fun Faire. Only the uneasy shimmering blue-white glare of the full moon, marking out the paths between the rides. A glowing maze, where the monster wasn't trapped in the centre any more. A slow breeze issued out of the arch, pressing against my face, cold as the grave.

Bad things had happened here, and perhaps were still happening, on some level. You can't kill that many people, spill that much blood, delight in that much suffering and slaughter, and not leave a stain on Time itself.

It all started out so well. The Fun Faire did have its share of unusual, high-risk, high-excitement attractions. Just the thing to tempt the jaded palates of Nightside aesthetes. Or perhaps even the worst of us need to play at being children again, just for a while. So, the Dodgems of Doom could hit Mach 2 and came equipped with mounted machine-guns. The planes on the Tilt-A-Wheel had heat-seeking missiles and ejector seats. The Ghost Train was operated by real ghosts, the Tunnel of Love by a real succubus. The roller coaster guaranteed to rotate you through at last five different spatial dimensions or your money back. And the candy floss came treated with a hundred and one different psychotropic drugs.

But eventually someone noticed that though an awful lot of people were going into Fun Faire, a significant percentage weren't coming out again.

And then it all went to Hell.

No-one's too sure what started it. Best guess is someone put a curse on the place, for whatever reason. The first clue that something was severely wrong came when the wooden horses on the Merry-Go-Round became possessed by demons and started eating their riders. The Tilt-A-Wheel speeded itself up and sent its mock planes shooting off into space. They didn't fly far. The roller coaster disappeared into another dimension, taking its passengers with it, and never returned. Distorted reflections burst out of the distorting mirrors and ran amok, killing everyone they could get their hands on.

Screams came out of the Ghost Train, and even worse screams out of the Tunnel of Love. The I-Speak-Your-Weight machines shouted out people's most terrible inner secrets. The Clown that never stopped laughing escaped from his booth and strode through Fun Faire, ripping off people's heads and hanging them from his belt. Still laughing. The customers ran for the exit. Some made it out.

The Authorities sealed off Fun Faire, so nothing inside could get out, and soon the whole place was dark and still and silent. No-one volunteered to go in and check for survivors, or bring out the dead. The Nightside isn't big on compassion.

The owners, and then their creditors, turned to priests

and exorcists, air strikes and high explosives, and none of it did any good. Fun Faire had become a Bad Place, and most people had enough sense to stay well clear of it. But, this being the Nightside, there were always those brave enough or stupid enough to use it as a hiding place, secure in the knowledge that only the most desperate pursuers would even think of coming in after them.

I looked at Suzie. "Fancy a stroll around? Check out all the fun of the fair?"

"Why not?" said Suzie.

We strode through the archway, shoulder to shoulder, into the face of the gusting breeze. It was bitterly cold inside the Faire, and the silence had a flat, oppressive presence. Our footsteps didn't echo at all. The rides and attractions loomed up around us, dark skeletal structures, and the rounded, almost organic shapes of the tattered tents and concession stands. We stuck to the middle of the moonlit paths. The shimmering light couldn't seem to penetrate the shadows. Here and there, things moved, always on the edge of my vision. Perhaps moved by the gusting wind, which seemed to be growing in strength. Suzie glared about her, shotgun at the ready. It might have been the oppressive nature of the place getting to her, or it might not. Suzie always believed in getting her retaliation in first.

We passed an old-fashioned I-Speak-Your-Weight machine, and I stopped and regarded it thoughtfully.

"I know a guy who collects these," I said, deliberately

casual. "He's trying to teach them to sing the 'Halleluiah Chorus.'"

"Why?" said Suzie.

"I'm not sure he's thought that far ahead," I admitted.

And then we broke off, as the machine stirred slowly into life before us. Parts moved inside it, grinding against each other, even though neither of us had stepped on it; and the voice-box made a low, groaning sound, as though it was in pain. The flat painted face lit up, sparking fitfully. And in a voice utterly devoid of humanity, or any human feeling, the machine spoke to us.

"John Taylor. No father, no mother. No family, no friends, no future. Hated and feared, never loved, or even appreciated. Why don't you just die and get it over with?"

"Not even close," I said calmly. "You'd probably get my weight wrong, too."

"Susan Shooter," said the voice. "Always the celibate, never the bride. No-one to touch you, ever. Not your breast, or your heart. You miss your brother, even though he sexually abused you as a child. Sometimes you dream of how it felt, when he touched you. No love for you, Susan. Not any kind of love, now or ever."

Suzie raised her shotgun and blew the painted face apart. The machine screamed once, and then was still. Suzie pumped another shell into the magazine. "Machines should know their place," she said.

"You can't trust anything you hear in Fun Faire," I said carefully. "The Devil always lies."

"Except when a truth can hurt you more."

"He doesn't know you like I do," I said. "I love you, Suzie."

"Why?"

"Somebody has to. There's a man for every woman, and a woman for every man. Just be glad we found each other."

"I am," said Suzie. And that was as far as she would go.

She spun round suddenly, her gun trained on one particular shadow. "Come out. Come out into the light where I can see you."

Max Maxwell emerged slowly and cautiously, even bigger in life than his ghost image had suggested. He held his huge hands up to show us they were empty, and then he smiled slowly, grey lips pulling back to show grey teeth.

"You're good, Suzie," he said, in a low, deep voice like stones grinding together. "No-one else would have known I was there."

"No-one sneaks up on me," said Suzie, her shotgun trained unwaveringly on his barrel chest. His cream suit looked somehow off in the moonlight, as though it had gone sour.

"I might have known they'd send you two," he said, apparently unmoved by the threat of the shotgun. "But I'm afraid you got here just a little too late. I didn't come here to hide; this whole place is a sink of other-dimensional energies, and the Aquarius Key has been soaking them up for hours. Soon the Key will be strong enough to open a door into the world of the loa; and then I will go through into that world . . . and the power stored in the Key will make me their master. A god of gods, lord of the loa."

"Really bad idea, Max," I said. "Messing with gods on their own territory. They'll eat your soul, one little bit at a time. What did you think you were doing, bringing them here and humiliating them?"

"It's wrong that we should be at their beck and call," said Max Maxwell, the Voodoo Apostate. "My people have worshipped them for centuries, and still the most we can hope for is that they will deign to ride us as their mounts. This is the Nightside. We have a Street full of gods, and we have taught them to know their place. As I will teach the loa."

He held out one hand towards me, and just like that, the Aquarius Key appeared upon it. The metal box looked like a toy on his huge pale palm. Its steel parts moved slowly against each other, sliding around and above each other, and I tried to look away, but I couldn't. The Key was becoming something actually uncomfortable to look at, as though it was rotating itself through strange, unfamiliar spatial dimensions, in search of the doorway into the world of the loa. It burst open, blossoming like a metal flower, and a wide split opened up in mid air, like a wound in reality.

A great sound filled the air, echoing through the silent forms of Fun Faire, like a cry of outrage. A bright light blasted out of the opening hanging on the air, so sharp

and fierce I had to look away, and just like that the spell
of the Key was broken. I fell back a pace, raising one arm
to shield my watering eyes against the fierce light. The
split in the night widened inexorably, sucking the air into
itself. It tugged at me, and at Suzie. I grabbed her waist,
as much to steady myself as hold her in place, and she was
steady as a rock, as always. Suzie grabbed on to the side of
the nearest ride, and I held on to Suzie as the pull in-
creased. Max Maxwell stood unaffected, protected by the
Aquarius Key, shuddering and twitching on the palm of
his hand. The rushing air shrieked as it was pulled into
the growing split in the air, along with everything else
loose. All kinds of junk flew through the air, tumbling
end over end. I was holding Suzie so tightly it must have
hurt her, but she never made a sound, and her white-
knuckled grip on the ride never faltered. She raised her
free hand, aimed the shotgun with one casual movement,
and shot the Aquarius Key right out of Max's hand.

He cried out in rage as much as pain, as his hand exploded in a flurry of flying blood and blown-away fingers.
The Key flew undamaged through the air, hit the ground,
and rolled away into the shadows. The long split in the air
slammed shut, and, just like that, the howling wind died
away to nothing. Max fell on all fours, ignoring the blood
that still spurted from his maimed hand, scrambling in
the shadows for the Key. I let go of Suzie's waist, and we
walked purposefully forward. Suzie chambered another
round, and Max rose suddenly, the Key raised triumphantly in his good hand. He snarled at me, and I

leaned forward and threw a handful of black pepper right into his face.

I never travel anywhere without condiments.

The pepper filled Max's eyes and nose, and he fell backwards, sneezing so hard it shook his whole body, while his eyes screwed shut around streaming tears. He couldn't even hold on to the Aquarius Key, let alone concentrate enough to operate it, and the metal box fell to the ground before him. So I just stooped down and took it away from him. Suzie nodded respectfully to me.

"You always did know the best ways to fight dirty."

She kicked Max briskly in the ribs with her steel-toed boot, just enough to take the fight out of him. He grunted once, and then glared up at us from his knees, forcing his watering eyes open. He was squeezing his injured hand with the other so tightly the bleeding had almost stopped. There were no signs of pain or weakness or even defeat in his dark face; only an implacable hatred, while he waited for his chance to come round again. Suzie shoved the barrel of her shotgun into his face.

"I get paid the same whether I bring you in dead or alive," she said, her voice cold and calm as always. "On the whole, I tend to prefer dead. Less paper-work."

"I am not carrying anyone that large out of here," I said firmly. "Unless I absolutely have to. So let's all play nice, then we can all walk out."

But Max wasn't listening to either of us. He was staring at something behind me, and even before he said anything, I could feel all the hackles on my neck rising.

"Ah, hell," said Max Maxwell. "Just when I thought things couldn't get any worse . . ."

Suzie and I turned to look, and there standing in rows behind us was a small army of the Nightside's very best bounty hunters. Heavily armed and armoured, they stood unnaturally still, all of them grinning unpleasantly, while their eyes glowed golden in the gloom, like so many candle-flames in the depths of Hell. Their wide grins showed teeth, like hunting dogs who'd brought their game to ground at last.

The loa had found us.

Max laughed suddenly, a flat, breathy sound. "Protect me, Suzie, Taylor. If you want your bounty money."

I looked at Suzie. "Do we really need the money that badly?"

"Always," said Suzie. "It isn't the principle of the thing, it's the money. No-one takes a bounty away from me."

"Maybe we could split him down the middle," I said.

"Tempting, but messy. And I don't share."

I sighed. "Things are in a bad way if I have to be the voice of reason . . ."

I stepped forward, conspicuously putting myself between the loa's hosts and their prey, and they all fixed their glowing unblinking eyes on me.

"We know you, John Taylor." It was hard to tell where the voice came from. It could have been any of them, or all of them. It sounded almost . . . amused. "We know who and what you are, probably better than you do yourself. But do not presume to stand between us and what is rightfully ours."

"And I know you, lords of the loa," I said, keeping my voice reasonably polite and respectful. "But this is my world, not yours, and Max is mine. He will be punished severely, I promise you."

"Not good enough," said the voice, and the whole possessed army surged forward as one.

Max reared up suddenly, catching me off guard. He snatched the Aquarius Key away from me with his one good hand and twisted it savagely, shouting Words of Power. And all the bounty hunters screamed, as the possessing loa were forced out of them. Dozens of men and women crumpled to the ground, twitching and shuddering and crying hot tears of relief. For a moment, I actually thought the threat was over. I should have known better.

All around me, all the old rides and machinery creaked slowly back into life, wheels turning, machinery stirring, while the wooden Merry-Go-Round horses slowly turned their heads to look at us. The loa had found new hosts. A slow, awful life moved through Fun Faire, burning fiercely inside cold metal and painted wood, and out of the mouths of oversized clowns and Tunnels of Love and Horror came the outraged screams of the defied loa.

Max was hunched over, struggling to manipulate the Aquarius Key with just the one good hand, trying to open a door that would take him away. Suzie clubbed him in the side of his head with the butt of her shotgun, and he hardly felt it. She hit him again, and while he was distracted I moved in and snatched the Key away. Max glared at me, grey lips pulling back to show grey teeth.

"I will kill you for this, Taylor. Make you crawl first; make her crawl. I'll let you watch helplessly as I violate your woman. Do her and do her till she bleeds, until her throat rips from screaming. Tear her apart, body and soul. I'll send her to Hell . . . and then it'll be your turn."

I looked at Suzie. "Kneecap him."

She blew off his left kneecap with her shotgun. His leg burst apart, blood spurting, and Max collapsed, crying out in agony as he clutched at his leg. I looked down at him.

"Shouldn't have threatened Suzie, Max. No-one messes with me and mine."

I turned my attention back to Fun Faire, coming slowly alive like a great beast stretching after a long sleep. Lights were snapping on all around us, flaring blue and green and pink in the dark. The huge rides creaked and groaned as rusting metal stirred to life again. Suzie moved in beside me, swinging her shotgun back and forth, restless for a target.

"John, what's happening?"

"The loa have possessed the whole damned fairground," I said. "All those exorcisms must have left it wide open . . ."

"Can't we get Max to throw them out again?"

"Possibly," I said. "If he wasn't currently preoccupied with holding his shattered leg together."

"It was your idea."

"I know, I know!"

The dodgem cars came first, smashing through the reinforced sides of their stand and heading straight for us at impossible speed. They hammered through the shadows, their wooden sides already splitting as they struggled to contain the terrible energies that were animating them. Suzie stood her ground and blasted the first car at point-blank range. It exploded in a shower of wooden spikes and splinters, some of which pattered harmlessly against the front of Suzie's motorcycle jacket. The rest of the dodgem cars were already upon us, so Suzie and I threw ourselves in opposite directions, out of their way. The cars swung round and over each other to come after us, their garishly painted faces grinning the same grin I'd seen on the faces of the possessed bounty hunters. The loa were having fun. The loa were playing with us.

I ran down the moonlit paths between the slowly stirring stands, and the cars came after me, calling out now in terrible voices. I could hear Suzie running, not far away, and yelled for her to intersect with me at the next crossing of the paths. We both arrived at the intersection at the same time, and I grabbed Suzie by the hand and pulled her to the ground. The cars came up on us too fast to stop, and flew right over our heads to slam into each other head-on. There was an explosion of splintered wood and released uncanny energies, and when Suzie and I scrambled to our feet again, their was nothing left of the dodgem cars but gaily painted wreckage.

"We need to get back to Max," said Suzie. She'd already pulled her hand out of mine, the moment we were safe. She couldn't bear to be touched for long, even when I was saving her.

"Max isn't going anywhere on that leg," I said.

"He could crawl," said Suzie.

So back we went, to face the loa again. I sometimes wonder which of us is crazier—Suzie for suggesting these things or me for going along with them.

She was right. We found Max at the end of a long bloody trail, crawling for the exit, dragging his useless leg behind him. We'd just caught up with him when the snub-nosed planes came flying down at us from the Tilt-A-Whirl. They'd broken free of their supporting struts and shot through the air towards us on stubby wooden wings. I just hoped someone had got around to removing the heat-seeking missiles. Suzie shot them out of the air, one by one, just like pigeon shooting. (There are no pigeons in the Nightside, and people like Suzie are the reason why. Sometimes you can't even find a dove to sacrifice when you're in a hurry.) The last plane crashed to the ground not five feet away from us and gave up its ghost. Suzie looked at me as she reloaded her shotgun.

"So? Do I win a prize?"

"Depends," I said. "You shoot horses, don't you?"

Suzie looked where I was looking and hurried her reloading. The carved wooden horses had dragged themselves free from the Merry-Go-Round and were heading our way. They were big and nasty and brightly coloured in places where paint still clung to the diseased wood. They had snarling rusty teeth in their grinning mouths, the hinged jaws working hungrily. Their eyes gleamed gold, just like the bounty hunters', and they stamped their heavy hoofs deep into the ground. And for all their rusty hinged joints, they moved very much like living things, driven by the wrath of the loa.

The old stories said the horses ate their riders; and right then I believed it.

"Now this is what I call a Fun Faire," said Suzie, and she opened fire with her shotgun.

The noise was deafening as she fired shell after shell, but though she hit every horse she aimed at, blowing huge chunks of wood out of them, they just kept coming. Suzie emptied her shotgun in under a minute and swore harshly as she scrambled at the bandoliers over her chest for reloads. The horses were very close now, but she still held her ground. The first wooden head lunged forward, and rusting teeth snapped shut on her black leather sleeve.

Which meant it was down to me, and one last desperate idea. I raised my gift and used it to find the last traces of the old magic that had once run the Faire, when it was still just an amusement park. Some last vestiges of that old innocent magic still remained, untouched by all the prayers and exorcisms, the evil and the horror, and I found it and put it back in touch with the wooden horses.

They stumbled to a halt, one by one, as the old magic stubbornly reinstated the terms of the original compact.

And one by one the horses were dragged back to the Merry-Go-Round. They fought it all the way, shaking their heads and stamping their heavy feet, but back they went. And as they stepped backwards up onto the Merry-Go-Round, the old steel poles slammed down again, piercing their wooden bodies through and holding them mercilessly in place.

I looked round at Suzie. She'd finished reloading her shotgun and was standing with one foot in the small of Max's back, to keep track of him. I nodded to her, and she took her boot away. I knelt down beside Max and helped him roll over onto his back. He was breathing hard, sweat beading all over his face, but he still glared unwaveringly up at me. I showed him the Aquarius Key in my hand.

"You know how to operate this, and I don't," I said carefully. "Use it and drive the loa out of Fun Faire. Use it for anything else, and Suzie will do to your head what she's already done to your knee."

He glared silently at me, but held out his good hand for the Key. I helped him sit up, then gave him the metal box. Suzie moved quickly forward to press the barrel of her shotgun against the back of his skull. He had to use what was left of his shattered hand in the end, despite the blood and the pain, but he made the Key do what he wanted, and a great cry went up all through Fun Faire as the loa were forced out. I quickly took the Key back again.

"John . . ." said Suzie. "Was this what you meant to happen?"

I looked where she was looking. The bounty hunters were back on their feet again, smiling their awful smiles, watching us with their glowing golden eyes. I had to sigh. Sometimes things wouldn't go right even if you bribed St. Peter. I moved forward to confront the bounty hunters, holding up the Aquarius Key so they could all see it. They stood very still, their glowing eyes fixed on me.

"When you were forced out of the rides, you were supposed to take the hint and go back where you came from," I said reproachfully.

"We won't go," they said, in their creepy single voice. "We can't go until we have satisfaction. And if you stand between us and our rightful vengeance, we will be at your back and at your throat for as long as you live."

I considered the problem. I could probably get Max to use the Key to send the loa home; but they'd just come back again, and again, till they got what they wanted. Max had hurt their pride, undermined their status as gods, and posed a threat to their whole religion. Hard to argue with that. It was an intriguing stand-off, and there was no telling which way it might have gone if Walker hadn't arrived. As usual he appeared out of nowhere, strolling casually out of the shadows as though he happened to be passing and thought he'd drop in for a chat. He came and stood beside me, and Suzie immediately moved to stand on my other side. Walker smiled easily at the ranks of possessed bounty hunters.

"Well, well, the gang's all here. But I think we've had

enough fun and games for one night. Max Maxwell is in my custody, and therefore under my protection. I can give you my word that he will be severely punished. I have a nice little cell just waiting for him, in Shadow Deep. And you know what we do to prisoners there."

"Not enough." One of the bounty hunters stepped forward to confront Walker. "Revenge, to be properly savoured, has to be personal. Has to be . . . hands-on."

"Not this time," said Walker. "This is the Nightside, and we deal with our own problems. *Go home.*"

He used the Voice on them. The Voice that cannot be disobeyed or opposed. It hammered on the air, so loud and forceful that even I winced. But the loa wouldn't budge. Until I raised my voice.

"Go home," I said. "Or I'll be very upset with you."

Perhaps I was bluffing. Perhaps not. I'll never tell. But it tipped the balance. They might have defied the powerful Walker or the infamous John Taylor, but not both of us at once. The bounty hunters collapsed again as the loa left them, returning at last to their own world. And that . . . was that. For now.

I looked at Walker. "You do know they'll be back, sometime. We hurt their feelings."

"Let them," said Walker. "They should have accepted a place on the Street of the Gods, when I offered it to them. There's no room for independent operators any more."

"Like me?" I said.

"Exactly."

I considered him thoughtfully. "Your Voice was impressive as always; but I can't help remembering it was granted to you by the Authorities. Who are all now extremely dead. So who powers your Voice these days?"

Walker smiled briefly. "I'm sure you'll find out, John. One of these days." He looked at Max Maxwell. *"Come with me."*

And shattered leg notwithstanding, Max Maxwell rose up and followed Walker out of Fun Faire, limping heavily all the way. The bounty hunters moved off after them, talking rather confusedly amongst themselves. Until only Suzie and I were left. She looked at me with her cold, utterly contained face.

"You saved my life, John. Again."

"And you saved mine," I said easily. "It's what we do. All part of being in a relationship."

"I know . . . it's not easy, for you," she said. "That close as we are, we still can't be . . . close. You've been so patient with me."

She reached out and touched my face gently with her fingertips. I stood very still and let her do it. I could feel the effort it took, for her to do that much. She trailed a fingertip across my lips—the closest we could come to a kiss. Suzie Shooter, Shotgun Suzie, who took no shit from me, or gods, or anyone in the Nightside, was still mostly helpless in the face of her own inner demons.

I would have killed the brother who'd done this to her if she hadn't already killed him years ago.

"I love you, Suzie," I said. "If you never believe anything else, believe that."

"I love you, John. As much as I can."

"That's what matters. That's all that matters."

"No it isn't!"

She made herself hug me, holding me tight. Her bandoliers of bracelets pressed against my chest. She was breathing hard, from the effort of what this cost her. Her whole body was stiff and tense. I didn't know whether to put my own arms around her or not, but in the end I held her as gently as I could.

"Love you, John," she said, her chin on my shoulder. I couldn't see her face. "Die for you. Kill for you. Love you till the world ends."

"I know," I said. "It's all right. Really."

But we both knew it wasn't.

# TWO

*Demon Girl Reporter*

Some days they won't even give you a chance to catch your breath. Suzie and I were just walking out of Fun Faire when my mobile phone rang. (The ring tone is the theme from *The Twilight Zone*. When I find a joke I like, I tend to stick with it.) An unctuous voice murmured in my ear.

"You have one phone call and one important message. Which would you like to hear first?"

"The call," I said determinedly.

"I'm sorry," said the voice. "I'm afraid I have been paid to insist you listen to the important message first. Have you ever considered the importance of good Afterlife insurance?"

I sighed, hit the exorcism function on the phone, and was gratified to hear the voice howl in pain as it was forced out of my phone. Admail . . . You'll never convince me it isn't a plot by demons from Hell to make life not worth living. With the admail banished, my call came through clearly. It was my teenage secretary, Cathy, calling from my office. (I'd rescued her from a house that ate people, and she adopted me. I didn't get a say in the matter. I let her run my office to keep her out of my hair. Worryingly, she's far better at it than I ever was.)

"Got a case for you, boss," she said cheerfully.

"I've just completed two in a row," I said plaintively. "I was looking forward to some serious quality time, with a nice hot bath and my rubber ducky. Rubber ducky is my friend."

"Oh, you'll want to take this one," said Cathy. "The offices of the one and only *Unnatural Inquirer* called. They need your services desperately, not to mention very urgently."

"What on earth does that appalling rag want with me? Or have they finally decided to hire someone to try to find their long-missing ethics and good taste?"

"Rather doubt it, boss. They wouldn't go into details over an open line, but they sounded pretty upset. And the money offered really is very good."

"How good?" I said immediately.

"Really quite staggeringly good," said Cathy. "Which means that not only are they pants-wettingly desperate, but there has to be one hell of a catch hidden away in it somewhere. Go on, boss, take the case. I'd love to hear what goes on in that place. They have all the best stories; I never miss an issue."

"The *Unnatural Inquirer* is a squalid, scabrous, tabloid disgrace," I said sternly. "And the truth is not in it."

"Who cares about truth, as long as they have all the latest gossip and embarrassing celebrity photos? Oh please please please . . ."

I looked at Suzie. "Do you need me to . . . ?"

"Go," she said. "I have to claim my bounty money."

She strode off, not looking back. Suzie's never been big on good-byes.

"All right," I said into the phone. "Give me the details."

"There aren't many. They want you to visit their editorial offices to discuss the matter."

"Why can't they come to my office?"

"Because you're never here. You have to come in soon, boss; I have a pile of paper-work that needs your signature."

"Go ahead and forge it for me," I said. "Like you did when you acquired those seven extra credit cards in my name."

"I said I was sorry!"

"Where do they want to meet?"

"They'll send someone to bring you to them. Employees of the *Unnatural Inquirer* don't like to be caught out in public. People throw things."

"Understandable," I said. "Where am I supposed to go, to be met?"

Cathy gave me directions to a particular street corner, in a not-too-sleazy area of the Nightside. I knew it: a busy place, with lots of people always passing through. A casual meeting stood a good chance of going unnoticed, lost in the crowd. I said good-bye to Cathy and shut down the phone before she could nag me about the paper-work again. If I'd wanted to shuffle papers for a living, I'd have shot myself in the head repeatedly.

Didn't take me long to get to the corner of Cheyne Walk and Wine Street, and I lurked as unobtrusively as possible in front of a trepanation franchise—Let Some Light In, Inc. Personally, I've always felt I needed trepanation like a hole in the head. Still, it made more sense than smart drinks ever did. People and others came and went, carefully minding their own business. Some stood out; a knight in shining armour with a miniature dragon perched on his steel shoulder, hissing at the passers-by; a fluorescent Muse, with Catherine-wheel eyes; and a sulky-looking Suicide Girl with a noose round her neck. But most were just people, familiar faces you wouldn't look twice at, come to the Nightside for the forbidden pleasures, secret knowledge, and terrible satisfactions they couldn't find anywhere else. The Nightside has always been something of a tourist trap.

I don't like standing around in the open. It makes me

feel vulnerable, an easy target. When I have to do surveillance, I always take pains to do it from somewhere dark and shadowy. People were starting to recognise me. Most gave me plenty of room; some nudged each other and stared curiously. One couple asked if they could take my photo. I gave them a look, and they hurried away.

To keep myself occupied, I went over what I knew about the *Unnatural Inquirer*. I'd read the odd copy; everyone has. People do like gossip, in the way we always like things that are bad for us. The Nightside has its own newspaper of record; that's the *Night Times*. The *Unnatural Inquirer*, on the other hand, has never allowed itself to be inhibited by mere facts. For them, the story is everything.

All the news that can be made to fit.

The *Unnatural Inquirer* has been around, in various formats, for over a hundred years, despite increasingly violent attempts to shut it down. These days Editorial, Publishing, and Printing all operate out of a separate and very private pocket dimension, hidden away behind layer upon layer of seriously heavy duty protections. You can get cursed down to the seventh generation just for trying to find it. The paper's defences are constantly being upgraded, because they have very powerful enemies. Partly because they print exaggerations, gossip, and outright lies about very important people, and partly because every now and again they tell the truth when no-one else will dare. The paper has no fear and shows no favour.

Only properly accredited staff can even approach the paper's offices. They're given special dimensional keys, bonded directly to the owner's soul, to prevent theft. The offices still get attacked on a daily basis. The paper prints details of every failed assault, just to rub it in. Despite everything the *Unnatural Inquirer* appears every day, full of things the rich and powerful would rather you didn't know about. There are no delivery trucks any more; they kept getting fire-bombed. New editions of the paper just appear out of nowhere, materialising right next to the news-stands all across the Nightside, direct from the printing presses. No-one ever interferes with the news-sellers; for fear of being lynched on the spot by the paper's fanatical audience.

And when you've finished reading the *Unnatural Inquirer*, just throw it away. It automatically disappears, returning to the printing presses to be recycled for the next edition. Even the *Night Times* can't match that. No-one has ever wrapped fish and chips in the *Unnatural Inquirer*.

On the other hand, the *Night Times*'s reporters and staff are on the whole well-known, respected, and admired. The *Unnatural Inquirer*'s people are often shot at on sight (especially the paparazzi), though if you survive long enough, you can end up as a (minor) celebrity. There's a high burn-out rate amongst the staff, but surprisingly there are always more, waiting in the wings to take their place. If you don't have it in you to be someone important or significant, or a celebrity, the next best thing is being someone who knows all about them and can crash all their parties.

"Hello, hello, John Taylor! Good to see you again, old thing! Still busy being infamous and enigmatic?"

I winced internally even as I turned to face the man who'd hailed me so cheerfully. I should have known who they'd send. Harry Fabulous was a fence and a fixer, and the best Go To man in the Nightside—for all those little and very expensive things that make life worth living. You want to smoke some prime Martian red weed, mainline some Hyde, or score someone else's childhood (innocence always goes down big in the Nightside), then Harry Fabulous is your man, always ready to take your last penny with a big smile and a hearty handshake.

Or at least he used to be. Apparently he'd had one of those life-changing experiences in the back room of a members-only club, and now he was more interested in doing Good Deeds. Before it was too late. There's nothing like a glimpse of Hell to jump-start a man's conscience.

Harry was dressed to kill, as always, looking slick and polished. He wore a long coat whose inside pockets were practically crammed with all sorts of things you might or might not want to spend too much money on. He had a long, thin face, a lean and hungry look, and dark, somewhat haunted, eyes. He smiled easily at me, a very practised smile, and I gave him something very similar in return.

We were both, after all, professionals.

"Didn't know you worked for the *Unnatural Inquirer*, Harry," I said.

"Oh, I'm just a stringer," he said vaguely. "I do get

around, and I have been known to hear things, so . . . I've been sent to bring you to their main offices, old thing. Sorry to keep you waiting, but I had to be sure you hadn't been followed."

"Harry," I said. "Remember who you're talking to."

"Oh, quite! Yes, indeed! Just a formality, really."

He fished inside his long coat and produced a very ordinary-looking key. He glanced round briefly, turned to face me to cover his movements, and pushed the key into an invisible lock, apparently floating in mid air between us. The key disappeared even as Harry turned it, and just like that the world seemed to drop away under my feet. There was a brief sensation of falling, and we left the Nightside behind us.

We reappeared in a Reception office that looked just like any other Reception office. Luxurious enough to impress on you how important the operation was, but not comfortable enough to encourage you to stick around any longer than was absolutely necessary. A cool blonde Receptionist sat behind a desk behind a layer of bulletproof glass. Manning the phones, doing maintenance on her fingernails, and dealing with visitors when she absolutely had to. Harry went to take my arm to usher me into the waiting area. I looked at him, and he quickly withdrew the hand. You can't let people like Harry Fabulous get too chummy; they take advantage. I strolled forward, looking curiously about me, and all the bells in the world went off at once.

"It's all right! It's all right!" yelled Harry, waving his arms and practically jumping up and down on the spot. "It's just John Taylor! He's expected!"

The bells shut off, and the Receptionist reappeared from underneath her desk, glaring venomously at Harry. I looked at him.

"Security scan," he said quickly. "Purely routine. Nothing to worry about. It's supposed to detect dangerous objects, and people, and you . . set off every alarm they have. I did warn them to dial down the settings while you were here . . . Would you like me to take your coat?"

"Wouldn't be wise," I said. "I haven't fed it recently."

Harry looked at me for some clue as to whether he was supposed to laugh, but I just looked right back at him. Harry swallowed hard, took a step back, and looked at the Receptionist.

"Contact Security, there's a dear, and tell them to make an exception for John Taylor."

"Make lots of them," I said. "I'm a very complicated person."

"I won't hang around," Harry decided. "I'm almost sure I'm urgently needed somewhere else."

He did the business with the key again and disappeared. That's Harry Fabulous for you. Always on the go.

The Receptionist and I looked at each other. Somehow I just knew we weren't going to get along. She was a small petite platinum blonde with sultry eyes, a mouth made for sin, and a general air of barely suppressed rage and violence. I didn't know whether that was a result of working here, or why they hired her in the first place. She was the first line of defence against anyone who turned up, and I had no doubt she had all kinds of interesting weapons and devices somewhere close at hand . . . I decided to be polite, for the moment, and gave her my best professional smile.

"My name is John Taylor. The Editor wants to see me."

She sniffed loudly and gave me a pitying smile. Her voice came clearly through the narrow grille in the bulletproof glass. "No-one ever sees the Editor. In fact, no-one's seen Mr. du Rois in the flesh for years. Safer that way. Your appointment will be with the Sub-Editor, Scoop Malloy."

"Scoop?" I said. "Was he one of your best reporters?"

"No; he used to work with animals. Take a seat."

I took a seat. I know when I'm outclassed. The long red leather couch was hard and unyielding. There was no-one else waiting in Reception. An assortment of old magazines were laid out on a low table. I leafed through them, but there was nothing particularly interesting. *Which Religion*'s cover boasted the start of a new series: *We road test ten new gods!* The Nightside edition of *Guns & Ammo* had Suzie Shooter on the cover again. They think she adds a touch of glamour. *What's on in the Nightside* was the size of a telephone directory. It's cover boasted *101 Things You Need to Know About Members Only Clubs! Including How to*

*Get In, and How to Get Out Alive Again*. I quite like *What's On*; it's constantly updating itself as people and places change and disappear. Sometimes the page will rewrite it-self even as you're reading it. They stopped having an index because it kept whimpering.

I gave up on the magazines, leaned back on the rock-hard sofa, and thought some more about what I knew about the *Unnatural Inquirer*'s legendary Editor, Owner, and Publisher, Gaylord du Rois. Everyone was pretty sure that wasn't his real name, but it had been right there at the top of the masthead of every issue for years now, right from the days when the photos were grainy black and white, the type-face was tiny, and they printed the whole thing on toilet paper. Gaylord might be a man, or a woman, or a committee. Might even have been several people in a row. No-one knew for sure, and it wasn't for want of trying to find out. Certainly the aggressive tone of the paper hadn't changed in over a hundred years; it was just as blunt and brash and obnoxious now as it had always been.

I sat more or less patiently on the couch, idly consid-ering the possibilities of redecorating the Reception area with a couple of incendiaries, while a handful of people drifted in and out. Reporters and office functionaries wandered past, caught up in their own business and pay-ing no attention at all to me. Paparazzi teleported in just long enough to drop off their latest snatched photos of celebrities doing things they shouldn't, and then disap-peared again. There are cannibal demons on the Street of the Gods less hated and despised than the *Unnatural Inquirer*'s paparazzi. Suzie shoots at them on sight, but so far she's only managed to wing a couple. We stopped them hanging about our house by planting disguised man-traps. Nothing like the occasional scream of a wounded paparazzi in the early hours of the morning to help you sleep peacefully.

A few of the paparazzi looked at me thoughtfully but were careful not even to point their cameras in my direction. It's all in the reputation.

"You're sure the Sub-Editor knows I'm waiting?" I said to the Receptionist. "I was told this was urgent."

"He knows," she said. "Or maybe he doesn't. Embrace the possibilities!"

I walked over to her and gave her one of my best hard looks. "I'll bet this place would burn up nicely if I put my mind to it."

"Go ahead. See if I care. The only time this place gets a makeover is after a good fire. Sometimes they just scrub down the walls."

I gave up. "Distract me. Talk to me. Tell me things."

"What sort of things?"

"Well, how big is the paper's circulation these days?"

She shrugged. "Don't think anyone knows for sure. The print run's been rising steadily for thirty years now, and it was huge before that. Sales aren't limited to the Nightside, you know. It goes out to all kinds of other worlds and dimensions. Because everyone's interested in what's happening in the Nightside. We get letters from all over. We got one from Mars."

"Really? What did it say?"

"No-one knows. It was in Martian."

I decided I didn't want to talk to her any more. I sat down on the couch again and looked at the framed front pages on the walls, showcasing the paper's long history.

*Elvis Really Is Dead! We Have Proof! Honeymoon Over; Giant Ape Admits Size Isn't Everything! Hitler Burns in Hell! Official! Orson Welles Was Really a Martian! We Have X-Rays! Our Greatest Ever Psychic Channels New Songs from Elvis, John Lennon, Marc Bolan, and Buddy Holly! All Available on a CD You Can Buy Exclusively from the* Unnatural Inquirer!

Proof, if proof were needed, that not only is there one born every second, but that they grow up to read the tabloids.

Still, if nothing else, the *Unnatural Inquirer* had style. It got your attention. For want of anything better to do, I picked up a copy of the latest edition from the low table. The front-page headline was *Tribute Four Horsemen of the Apocalypse to Tour Nightside! Over Their Dead Bodies, Says Walker!* I leafed through the paper, grimacing as the cheap print came off on my fingers.

Apparently the Holy Order of Saint Strontium had been forcibly evicted from the Street of the Gods after it was discovered that their Church had a radioactive half-life of two million years. "Bunch of pussies," said Saint Strontium. He had a lot more to say, but none of the reporters present wanted to hang around long enough to find out what . . . There were some intriguing Before and After photos of Jacqueline Hyde, poor soul. Jacqueline and Hyde were in love, but doomed never to meet save for the most fleeting of moments . . . Another story insisted that the Moon really was made of green cheese, and that the big black monoliths were just oversized alien crackers . . . And right at the bottom of an inner page, in very small type: *Old Ones Fail to Rise Yet Again.*

Most of the rest of the pages were filled with excited puff pieces about various Nightside celebrities I either hadn't heard of, or didn't give a damn about, including two whole pages given over to photos of young women getting out of limousines and taxis, just so the paparazzi could get a quick photo of their underwear, or lack of it. As far as the *Unnatural Inquirer* is concerned, taste is something you find in the restaurant guides.

I skipped through to the personal ads and announcements in the back pages; all human life is there, and a whole lot more besides.

Soul-swapping parties; just show up and throw your karma keys into the circle. Bodies for rent. Sex change while you wait. Go deep-sea diving in sunken R'lyeh; no noise-makers allowed. A whole bunch of pyramid schemes, some involving real pyramids. Remote viewing into the bedrooms and bathrooms of the rich and famous; highlights available on VHS or DVD. Time-share schemes, involving real time travel. (Though those tended to be stamped on pretty quick by Old Father Time, especially if they weren't cons.) And, of course, a million different drugs from thousands of dimensions; buyer very much beware. The paper felt obliged to add its own warning here; apparently some intelligent plant civilisations had been attempting to stealthily invade our world by selling their seeds and cuttings as drugs. Sort of a Trojan horse invasion . . .

And then, of course, there were the personal messages . . . *Lassie come home, or the kid gets it. Boopsie loves Moopsie; Moopsie loves Boopsie?* (Oh, I could see tears before bedtime in the offing there . . . ) *Dagon shall rise again! All donations welcome. Desperately Seeking Elvira . . . Mad scientist who digs up graves, steals the bodies, and sews the bits together to create a new living supercreature seeks similar . . . GSOH essential.*

The *Unnatural Inquirer* has the only crossword puzzles that insult you if you take too long at guessing the clues—very cross word puzzles. And they had to cancel the kakuro because the numbers kept adding up to 666.

I dropped the paper back onto the table, went to wipe my inky fingers on my coat, and then realised that's not a good idea when you're wearing a white trench coat. I took out a handkerchief and rubbed briskly at my fingers. I hadn't realised how much I knew about the paper. The tabloid had insinuated itself into the Nightside so thoroughly that pretty much anything you saw or thought of reminded you of something that had appeared in the *Unnatural Inquirer*. For a while there was even a rumour going around that the Editor had a precog on staff, who could see just far enough into the future to view the next day's edition of the *Night Times*, so that the *Unnatural Inquirer* could run all their best stories in advance. I had trouble believing that. First, I knew the Editor of the *Night Times*, and he wouldn't sit still for something like that for one moment, and second, the *Unnatural Inquirer* had never been that interested in news stories anyway. Not when there's important gossip and tittle-tattle to spread.

Not that the *Unnatural Inquirer* gets everything its own way. The Editor once sent a reporter into Rats' Alley, where the homeless and down-and-outs gather, to dig up some juicy stories on rich and famous people who'd been brought low by misfortune and disaster. Razor Eddie, Punk God of the Straight Razor, and defenders of street people everywhere, rather took exception to such hardheartedness. He sent the reporter back to the Editor in forty-seven separate parcels. With postage owing.

"The Sub-Editor is ready to see you now," said the Receptionist. "He's sending a copy-boy to escort you in."

"Does he think I'll get lost?" I said.

She smiled coldly. "We don't like people wandering around. Personally, I think all visitors should be electronically tagged and stamped with time codes so they'd know exactly when their welcome was wearing out."

The door to the inner offices opened, and out shambled a hunched and scowling adolescent in a grubby T-shirt and jeans. His T-shirt bore the legend FUCK THEM ALL AND LET THE DOCTORS SORT THEM OUT. He flicked his long, lank hair back out of his sullen face, looked me over, grunted once, and gestured for me to follow him inside. I felt like giving him a good slap, on general principles.

"Let me guess," I said. "Everything's rotten and nothing's fair."

"I'm nineteen!" he said, glaring at me dangerously. "Nineteen, and still a copy-boy! And I've got qualifications . . . I'm being held back. You just wait; there'll be some changes made around here once they finally see sense and put me in charge . . ."

"What's your name?" I said.

"I'm beginning to think it's *Hey you!* That's all I ever hear in this place. Like it would kill the old farts that work here to remember my name. Which is Jimmy, if you really care, which you probably don't."

"And what do you want to be when you grow up?" I said kindly.

His glare actually intensified, and veins stood out in his neck. "To be a reporter, of course! So I can dig up the secrets of the rich and powerful, and then blackmail them." He looked at me slyly. "I could always start with you. Get a good story on the infamous and mysterious John Taylor, and they'd have to give me my own by-line. Go on; tell me something really shocking and sordid about you and Shotgun Suzie. Does she really take the gun to bed with her? Do you sometimes swap clothes? You'd better give me something, or I'll just make up something really juicy and extra nasty anyway. I'll say you said it, and it'll be just your word against mine."

I looked at him thoughtfully, and he fell back a step. "Jimmy," I said, "if I see one word about Suzie or me in this rag with your name on it, I will use my gift to find you. And then I'll send Suzie to you, who will no doubt wish to demonstrate her extreme displeasure. Suddenly and violently and all over the place."

He sniffed dismally. "Worth a try. Follow me. Sir."

He led me into the inner offices of the *Unnatural Inquirer*. The air was thick with cigarette smoke, incense, sweat, and tension. People bustled importantly back and forth around the various reporters, who were all working with furious concentration at their desks, hammering their computer keys like their lives depended on it. They kept calling out to each other, mostly without looking up from what they were doing, demanding information, opinions, and the very latest gossip, like so many ravenous baby birds in a nest. They all sounded cheerful enough, but there was a definite undercurrent of malice and cut-throat competition. The general noise level was appalling, the air was almost unbreathable, and the whole place seethed with talent and ambition.

It was everything I'd hoped it would be.

The copy-boy slouched down the main central aisle with me in tow, and everyone ostentatiously ignored me. There was a definite bunker atmosphere to the inner offices; probably because most people really were out to get them, for one reason or another. The industrious men and women of the *Unnatural Inquirer* drank and smoked like it was their last day on Earth, because it just might be.

Their readers might love them, but nobody else did. For the staff here it was always going to be Us versus Them, with everything and everyone fair game. There were always lawsuits, but the Editor & Publisher could afford the very best lawyers and took pride in keeping cases in court forever and a day. The paper might never have won a case, but it had never lost one either, mostly because the paper outspent or outlived the litigants. The *Unnatural Inquirer* had never once apologised, never printed a retraction, and never paid a penny in compensation. And was proud of it. Which was why the staff had to hide away in a bunker and take out special insurance against assassination attempts.

There was a prominent sign on one wall. YOU DON'T HAVE TO BE VICIOUS, PETTY-MINDED, AND MEAN-SPIRITED TO WORK HERE; BUT IT HELPS. Anywhere else, this would have been a joke.

Jimmy the copy-boy finally brought me to the Sub Editor's office, knocked on the door like he was announcing the imminent arrival of the barbarian hordes, and pushed the door open without waiting for a reply. I followed him in, shutting the door carefully behind me, and Scoop Malloy himself stood up from behind his paper-scattered desk to greet me. He was a short, dumpy figure, with a sad face and a prematurely bald head, wearing a pullover with the phrase SMILE WHEN YOU CALL ME THAT embroidered over his chest. He popped a handful of little purple pills from a handy bottle, dry-swallowed them in one, and came out from behind his desk to give me a limp, almost apologetic handshake. I shook his hand gingerly. Partly because I was remembering where his nickname came from, and partly because his hand felt like it might come off in mine.

He glared at the copy-boy. "What are you still doing here? Isn't there some important tea you should be making?"

"Fascist!" Jimmy hissed, slamming the door behind him on his way out. Then he opened it again, shouted, "I'm nineteen! Nineteen!" and disappeared again.

Scoop Malloy sighed deeply, sat down behind his desk, and gestured for me to take the visitor's chair. Which was, of course, hard and uncomfortable, as visitor's chairs always are. I think it's supposed to imply you're only there on sufferance.

"Puberty's a terrible thing," said Scoop. "Particularly for other people. I'd fire him if he wasn't someone's nephew . . . Wish I knew whose . . . Welcome to the salt mines, Mr. Taylor. Sorry to drag you all the way in here, but you see how it is. The price of freedom of the Press is eternal vigilance and constant access to heavy-duty armaments."

"I was given to understand that the matter was urgent," I said. "And that the pay would be quite staggeringly good."

"Oh, quite," said Scoop. "Quite." He looked at me searchingly. "I understand you've done some work for Julien Advent, at the *Night Times*."

"On occasion," I said. "I approve of Julien."

Scoop smirked unpleasantly. "I could tell you some things about him . . ."

"Don't," I said firmly. "First, I wouldn't believe them; and second, if you were to insult my good friend Julien Advent, I would then find it necessary to beat you severely about the head and shoulders. Quite probably until your head came off, after which I would play football with it up and down the inner offices."

"I never believed those stories anyway," Scoop said firmly. He leaned forward across his desk, trying hard to look business-like. "Mr. Taylor, here at the *Unnatural Inquirer* we are not in the news business, as such. No. We print stories, entertainment, a moment's diversion. We employ a manic depressive to write the Horoscopes; to keep our readers on their toes, we run competitions with really big prizes, like *Guess where the next Timeslip's going to appear*; and we're always first with news about what the rich and famous are up to. Even if that news isn't exactly accurate. We print the stories people want to read."

"And to Hell with whether they're true?" I said.

Scoop shrugged, smiling his unpleasant smile again. "Oh, you'd be surprised how close to the truth we get, even if it is by accident."

There was a knock at the door. Scoop looked up with a certain amount of relief that he wouldn't have to face me alone any more. He called for the new arrival to enter, the door opened, and both Scoop and I stood up to greet the newcomer. She was tall and athletic-looking, and drop-dead gorgeous. Long jet-black hair framed a heart-shaped face, with high cheek-bones, sparkling eyes, and one of those old-fashioned pouting rosebud mouths. She wore a smart polka-dot dress, carefully cut to show off as much of her excellent body and magnificent bosom as possible.

She also had two cute little horns curling up from her forehead, poking out of her Bettie-Page-style bangs.

"This is one of our most promising young journalists," Scoop said proudly. "John Taylor, may I present to you Bettie Divine. And vice versa, of course. She'll be partnering you on this case."

I'd been reaching out to shake Bettie's hand, but immediately withdrew it. I glared at Scoop.

"I don't think so. I choose my own partners on cases, people I know can keep up with me and look after themselves. I can't guarantee you results if I have to drag a passenger around with me. No offence, Bettie."

"None taken," she said cheerfully in a rich husky voice. "But I work for the *Unnatural Inquirer*. Let's see if you can keep up with me."

She sat on the edge of the Sub-Editor's desk, crossing her legs to show off an awful lot of thigh, and leaning back so she could arch her back and point her breasts at me. Good tactics. Good legs. Really good breasts.

"Hey," she said, amused. "My face is up here."

"So it is," I said. "What exactly is it you do here, Bettie?"

"I am a demon girl reporter, darling. And I do mean demon. Daddy was a Rolling Stone, on one of their Nightside tours, Mummy was a slut lust demon groupie.

Somebody ought to have known better, but here I am. Large as life, and twice as talented. I really am a first-class journalist, and you're going to need me on this case, darling. So, just lie back and enjoy it."

"She's right," Scoop said heavily. He sat down behind his desk again, and I lowered myself back onto the unwelcoming visitor's chair. Scoop laced his fingers together and looked at me steadily. "Bettie's accompanying you is part of the deal, Mr. Taylor. If we've got to spend the kind of money it's going to take to get you to do this for us, we are determined to get our money's worth. And the best way to recoup some of the expense is by running our very own exclusive story of how you did it."

"*On the case with John Taylor!*" said Bettie. "*An intimate account of our time together, traversing the darkest depths of the Nightside!* Honestly, sweetie, we won't be able to print copies fast enough. The bouncer might as well be outside throwing them in. No-one's ever had a story like this."

"No," I said.

She slid forward off the desk and leaned over me, so close I could feel her breath on my face. "You're going to need me on this case, darling. Really you are. And I can be very helpful."

I stood up, and she retreated a little. "Put the brakes on, *darling*," I said. "I'm spoken for."

"Ah, yes!" said Bettie, clapping her dainty little hands together and giving me a knowing look. "We know all about that! The infamous John Taylor and the sexy psycho killer Shotgun Suzie! We're already taking odds as to which of you will end up killing the other. Do tell us all about her, John; what's Suzie really like? Is she still sexy when the bedroom door is shut? What do you talk about in those special little moments? Inquiring minds are positively panting to know all the sordid little details!"

"Let them pant," I said, and something in my voice made her fall back a step. "Suzie is a very private, very dangerous person."

"Why don't I explain exactly what the case entails," Scoop said quickly. I sat down in my chair again, and Bettie leaned against the side of the desk, facing me, her arms folded under her impressive bosom. I concentrated on Scoop.

"There has been a broadcast from the Afterlife," Scoop said bluntly. "And the broadcast has been intercepted. It turned up on someone's television set, quite out of the blue with no warning; and the possessor of that television set, one Pen Donavon, was sharp enough to record it, and burn it onto a DVD. He then approached us, offering the Afterlife Recording for sale; and we bought exclusive rights to it for one hell of a lot of money."

"An intercepted broadcast?" I said. "From Heaven, or Hell?"

"Who knows?" said Scoop. "For that matter, who cares? This is actual information, from the Great Beyond! Our readers will eat this up with spoons."

"Am I to understand you haven't actually seen what's on this DVD yet?" I said.

"Not a glimpse," Scoop said cheerfully.

"It could be a fake," I said. "Or it could be a broadcast from some other world or dimension."

"Doesn't matter," said Scoop. "We own it. We want it. But unfortunately, Donavon has disappeared. He was on his way to us, with the DVD, in return for the very generous cheque we had waiting, but he never got here. We want you to find it, and him, for us. We have to have that Recording! We've been trailing it all week, for its appearance in the Sunday edition! If someone else gets their hands on it, and pips us to the post . . . And it's not just the story; do you have any idea how much we could make selling copies of the DVD?"

I was still unconvinced, despite his enthusiasm. "This isn't going to be like that transmission from the future that someone taped off their television back in the nineties, is it? Suzie bought a copy of the tape off eBay, and when we played it, it was only a guy in a futuristic outfit, showing his bare arse to the camera and giggling a lot."

Scoop leaned forward over his desk, doing his best to fix me with his watery eyes. "The *Unnatural Inquirer* authorises you to find and recover this Afterlife Recording, and its owner, by any and all means you deem necessary. Bring the DVD to us, preferably with the owner but not necessarily, and the *Unnatural Inquirer* will pay you one million pounds. In cash, gold, diamonds, or postage stamps; whatever you prefer. We'll also pay you a bonus of another fifty thousand pounds, if you will agree to watch the Recording and give us your expert opinion as to whether or not it's the real thing. The word is, you are qualified to know."

I nodded, neither confirming nor denying. "And if I say it's a fake?"

Scoop shrugged. "We'll put it out anyway. We can always spice it up with some specially shot extra footage. We can use the same people we've got working on Lilith's diaries."

"Wait just a minute!" I said. "I know for a fact that my mother never left any diaries!"

"We know!" said Scoop. "That's why we've got three of our best people writing them now, in the next room. They're going to be big, I can tell you! Not as big as the Afterlife Recording, of course, which will be a license to print money . . . Not that we'd do that, of course. Not after the last time . . . You have to find this DVD for us!"

"And I go along with you to tell the story of how you tracked it down!" said Bettie.

I thought about it. A million pounds was an awful lot of money . . . "All right," I said. "Partner."

Bettie Divine jumped up and down, and did a little dance of joy, which did very interesting things to her breasts. I looked back at Scoop.

"If this Afterlife Recording should turn out to be the real thing," I said, "I'm not sure anyone should be allowed to see it. Real proof of Heaven or Hell? I don't think we're ready for that."

"It's the headline that's important," said Scoop. "That's

what will sell lots and lots of papers. The DVD . . . can be fixed, one way or the other. It's the concept we're selling."

"But if it is real," I said. "If it is hard evidence of what happens after we die . . . the whole Nightside could go crazy."

"I know!" said Bettie Divine. "A real story at last! Who would have thought it! Isn't it simply too wonderful, darling!"

# THREE

*Faith, Hope, and Merchandising*

Bettie and I stepped out of the *Unnatural Inquirer*'s offices and shot straight back to the same street corner I'd left, appearing abruptly out of nowhere thanks to Bettie's dimensional key. No-one paid us any attention. People appearing out of nowhere is business as usual in the Nightside. It's when people start disappearing suddenly that everyone tends to start screaming and taking to their heels, and usually with good reason. I realised Bettie was looking at me expectantly, and I sighed inwardly. I knew that look.

"I know that look," I said to her sternly. "You've heard all the stories, studied up on the legend, and now you expect me to solve the whole case with one snap of my fingers. Probably while smiling sardonically and saying something wickedly witty and quotable. Sorry, but it doesn't work that way."

"But . . . everyone knows you have a gift!" said Bettie, fixing me with her big dark eyes like a disappointed puppy. "You can find anyone, or anything. Can't you?"

"You of all people should know better than to believe in legends," I said. "Reality is always far more complicated. Case in point: yes, I do have a gift for finding things, and people, but I can't just use it to pinpoint the exact location of Pen Donavon or his DVD. I need a specific question to get a specific answer. But with the information I've got, I should be able to get a rough sense of where to start looking . . ."

I concentrated, waking my third eye, my private eye, and the world started to open up and reveal its secrets to me . . . and then I cried out in shock and pain as a sudden harsh pressure shot through my head, slamming my inner eye shut. Some great force from Outside had shut down my gift as quickly and casually as a dog shrugging off a bothersome flea. I swore harshly, and Bettie actually retreated a couple of steps.

"Sorry," I said, trying to ease the scowl I could feel darkening my face. "Something just happened. It would appear that Someone or Something big and nasty doesn't want me using my gift. They've shut me down. I can't See a damned thing."

"I didn't know anyone could do that," said Bettie.

"It's not something I'm keen to advertise," I said. "Has

to be a Major Player of some kind. I hope it's not the Devil again . . ."

"*Again?*" said Bettie delightedly. "Oh, John, you do lead such a fascinating life! Tell me all about it!"

"Not a chance in Hell," I said. "I don't discuss other client's cases. Anyway, it's not like I'm helpless without my gift. We'll have to do this the old-fashioned way: asking questions, following leads, and tracking down clues."

"But . . . if a Major Player is involved, doesn't that mean the Afterlife Recording must be the real deal?" said Bettie. "Or else, why would they get involved?"

"They're involved for the same reason we are," I said. "Because they want to discover whether the Recording is the real deal, or not. Or . . . because Someone wants us to think it's real . . . Nothing's ever simple in the Nightside."

And then I stopped and looked thoughtfully at Bettie Divine. There was something subtly different about her. Some small but definite change in her appearance since we'd left the *Unnatural Inquirer* offices. It took me a moment to realise she was now wearing a large floppy hat.

"Ah," said Bettie. "You've noticed. The details of my appearance are always changing. Part of my natural glamour, as the daughter of a succubus. Don't let it throw you, dear; I'm always the same underneath."

"How very reassuring," I said. "We need somewhere quiet, to think and talk this through . . . somewhere no-one will bother us. Got it. The Hawk's Wind Bar and Grille isn't far from here."

"I know it!" said Bettie, clapping her little hands together delightedly. "The spirit of the sixties! Groovy,
baby!"

"You're like this all the time, aren't you?" I said.

"Of course!"

"I will make your Editor pay for this . . ."

"Lot of people say that," said Bettie Divine.


The Hawk's Wind Bar & Grille started out as a swinging
café and social watering hole for all the brightest lights of
the 1960s. Everyone who was anyone made the scene at
the Hawk's Wind, to plot and deal and spread the latest
gossip. It was wild and fabulous, and almost too influential for its own good. It burned down in 1970, possibly
self-immolation in protest at the splitting up of the
Beatles, but it was too loved and revered to stay dead for
long. It came back as a ghost, the spirit of a building
haunting its own location. People's belief keeps it real and
solid, and these days it serves as a repository for all that
was best of the sixties.

You can get brands of drink and food and music that
haven't existed for forty years in the rest of the world at
the Hawk's Wind Bar & Grille, and famous people from
the sixties are always dropping in, through various forms
of Time travel, and other less straightforward means. It's
not for everyone, but then, what is?

I pushed open the Hindu latticed front door and led
the way in. Bettie gasped and oohed at the psychedelic

patterns on the walls, the rococo Day-Glo neon signs, and the Pop Art posters of Jimi, Che, and Timothy Leary. The air was thick with the scents of jasmine, joss sticks, and what used to be called jazz cigarettes. A complicated steel contraption hissed loudly in one corner as it pumped out several different colours of steam and dispensed brands of coffee with enough caffeine to blow the top of your head clean off. Hawk's Wind coffee could wake the dead, or at least keep them dancing for hours. I sat Bettie down at one of the Formica-covered tables and lowered myself cautiously onto the rickety plastic chair.

Revolving coloured lights made pretty patterns across walls daubed in swirls of primary colours, while a jukebox the size of a Tardis pumped out one groovy hit after another, currently the Four Tops' "Reach Out, I'll Be There." Which has always sounded just a bit sinister to me, for a love song. All around us sat famous faces from the Past, Present, and Futures, most there to just dig the scene. Bettie swivelled back and forth in her chair, trying to take it all in at once.

"Don't stare," I said. "People will think you're a reporter."

"But this is so *amazing!*" said Bettie, all but bouncing up and down in her chair. "I've never been here before. Heard about it, of course, but . . . people like me never get to come to places like this. We only get to write about them. Didn't I hear this place had been destroyed?"

"Oh, yes," I said. "Several times. But it always comes

back. You can't keep a good ghost down, not when so many people believe in it."

The juke-box's music changed to Manfred Mann's "Ha! Ha! Said the Clown." Go-Go girls, wearing only handfuls of glued-on sequins, danced wildly in golden cages suspended from the ceiling. At a nearby table, a collection of secret agents exchanged passwords and cheerful tall tales, while playing ostentatiously casual one-upmanship with their latest gadgets—pens and shoes that were communication devices, watches that held strangling wires and lasers, umbrellas that were also sword-sticks. One agent actually blinked on and off as he demonstrated his invisibility bracelet. Not far away, the Travelling Doctor, the Strange Doctor, and the Druid Doctor were deep in conference. Presumably some Cosmic Maguffin had gone missing again. And there were the King and Queen of America, smiling and waving, as they passed through.

A tall and splendid waitress dressed in a collection of pink plastic straps and thigh-high white plastic boots strode over to our table to take our order. Her impressive bust bore a name badge with the initials EV. She leaned forward over the table, the better to show off her amazing cleavage.

"Save it for the tourists, Phred," I said kindly. "What are you doing working here? The monster-hunting business gone slack?"

She shrugged prettily. "You know how it is, John. My work is always seasonal, and a girl has to eat. You wait till the trolls start swarming again in the Underground and see how fast they remember my phone number. Now, what can I do you for? We've got this amazing green tea in from Tibet, though it's a bit greasy; or we've got some freshly baked fudge brownies that will not only open your doors of perception, but blow the bloody things right off their hinges."

"Just two Cokes," I said firmly.

"You want curly-wurly straws with that?"

"Of course," I said. "It's all part of the experience."

"Excuse me," said Bettie, "but why does he call you Phred, when your initials are EV? What does the EV stand for?"

"Ex-Virgin," said Phred. "And I stand for pretty much anything."

And off she went to get our order, swaying her hips through the packed tables perhaps just a little more than was strictly necessary.

"You know the most interesting people, John," said Bettie.

I grinned. "Let us concentrate on the matter at hand. What can you tell me about the guy who originally offered to sell you the Afterlife Recording?"

"All anyone knows is the name, Pen Donavon," said Bettie, frowning prettily as she concentrated. "No-one in the offices has ever met him; our only contact has been by phone. He called out of the blue and almost got turned away. We get a lot of crank calls. But he was very insistent, and once we realised he was serious, he got bumped up to Scoop, who in turn passed him on to the Editor, who made the deal for exclusive rights."

"For a whole lot of money," I said. "Doesn't that strike you as odd, given that no-one ever met Donavon, or even glimpsed what was on the DVD?"

"We had to pin the rights down before he went somewhere else! Trust me, the paper will make more money out of this story than Donavon will ever see."

"Do you at least have his address?"

"Of course!" Bettie said indignantly. "We've already checked; he isn't there. Skipped yesterday, owing two weeks' rent."

"We need to go there anyway," I said patiently. "There may be clues."

"Ooh, *clues*!" Bettie said delightedly. "Goody! I've never seen a clue."

She opened up a large leather purse, which I would have sworn she wasn't carrying before, and rummaged around in it for her address book. The purse seemed to be very full and packed with all kinds of interesting things. Bettie caught me looking, and grinned.

"Mace spray, with added holy water. Skeleton keys, including some made from real bones. And a couple of smoke grenades, to cover a quick exit. A demon girl reporter has to be prepared for all kinds of things, sweetie."

We went to Pen Donavon's place. It wasn't far. Bettie stuck close beside me. She wasn't too keen on appearing in public, given some of the stories she'd written. Apparently while celebrities tended to take such things in their stride, their fans could be downright dangerous.

"Relax," I said. "No-one's going to look at you while I'm here."

"You do seem to attract a lot of attention," Bettie agreed, peering out from under her large floppy hat, which was now a completely different colour. "It's really fascinating, the way people react to your presence. I mean, there's fear, obviously, and even an element of panic; but some people look at you in awe, as though you were a king, or a god. You really have done most of the things people say, haven't you?"

"I shall neither confirm nor deny," I said. "Let's just say I get around, and leave it at that."

"And you and Shotgun Suzie . . . ?"

"Are off-limits. Don't go there."

She smiled at me dazzlingly. "Can't blame a girl for trying, darling."

It turned out Pen Donavon had a small apartment over a pokey little junk shop, one more in a row of shabby, grubby establishments offering the usual dreams and damnations at knocked-down prices. The kind of area where the potential customers scurry along with their heads bowed, so they won't have to make eye contact with anyone. Pen Donavon's establishment boasted the grandiose name *Objets du Temps Perdu*, a literary allusion that was no doubt wasted on most of his clientele. I wasn't entirely sure I got it myself.

Bettie and I peered through the streaky, fly-specked window. It appeared that Donavon specialised in the kind of weird shit that turns up in the Nightside, through the various Timeslips that are always opening and closing. Lost objects and strange artifacts, from other times and dimensions. All the obviously useful, valuable, or powerful things are snapped up the moment they appear; in fact, there are those who make a good living scavenging the Timeslips. (Though they have to be quick on their feet; there's never any telling how long a Timeslip will last, and you don't want to be caught inside it when it disappears.) But a lot of what appears often defies easy description, or analysis, and such things tend to trickle down through the mercantile community, the price dropping at every stage, until it ends up in shops like these. Things too intricate, too futuristic, or just too damned weird to be categorised, even by all the many learned authorities that the Nightside attracts like a dog gets fleas. Great discoveries, and fortunes, have been made in places like this. But not many.

I rubbed the sleeve of my trench coat against the window. It didn't help.

"Well," I said. "Nothing here to give the Collector any sleepless nights. Only the usual junk and debris from the various time-lines. I wouldn't give you tuppence for any of it."

"Wait a minute," said Bettie. "You know the Collector? Personally? Wow . . . I keep forgetting, you know all the legends of the Nightside. What's he like?"

"Vain, obsessive, and very dangerous," I said.

"Oh, that is so cool. I never get to meet any legends. I just write about them."

"Best way," I said. "They'd only disappoint you in person."

"Like you?" said Bettie.

"Exactly."

The window display did its best to show off odd bits of future technology, most of which might or might not have been entirely complete, along with oddly shaped things that might have been Objects of Power, alien artifacts or relics of lost histories. Carpets that might fly, eggs that might hatch, puzzle-boxes that might open if only you could find the right operating Words. No price tags on anything, of course. Bargaining was everything, in a place like this.

The sign on the door said CLOSED. I tried the door, and it opened easily. No bell rang as we entered. There was no sign of any shop assistant, or customers, and the state of the place suggested there hadn't been any for some time. The gloomy interior was so still and silent you could practically hear the dust falling. I called out, in case anyone might still be skulking somewhere, but no-one answered. My voice sounded flat in the quiet, as though the nature of the place discouraged loud noises. Bettie dubiously studied some of the things set out on glass shelves, wrinkling her perfect nose at some of the more organic specimens, while I went behind the counter to check out the till. It was the old-fashioned type, with heavy brass push keys, and pop-up prices. It opened easily, revealing drawers empty save for a handful of change. Beside the till was a letter spike with piled-up bills. I checked through them quickly; they weren't so much bills as final demands, complete with threats and menaces. Clearly the shop had not been doing well.

A man with this kind of economic pressure hanging over him might well see a way out through fabricating an Afterlife Recording, and then lose his nerve when the time came to actually present it to the *Unnatural Inquirer*.

I found a set of stairs at the back, leading up to the overhead apartment. I insisted on going first, just in case, and Bettie crowded my back all the way up. The bare wooden steps creaked loudly, giving plenty of advance warning, but when we got to the apartment the door was already slightly ajar. I made Bettie stand back and pushed the door open with one hand. The room beyond was silent and empty of life. I stepped inside and stood by the door, looking around thoughtfully. Bettie pushed straight past me and darted round the place, checking all the rooms. No-one was home. Pen Donavon's apartment was a dump, with the various sad pieces of his life scattered everywhere. There were no obvious signs that the place had already been searched. It would have been hard to tell.

The furniture was cheap and nasty, the carpet was threadbare, and the single electric light bulb didn't even have a shade. And yet the main room was dominated by a huge wide-screen television, to which had been bolted a whole bunch of assorted unfamiliar technology. The additions stood out awkwardly, with trailing wires and spiky antennae. Some of it looked like future tech, some of it alien. Lights glowed here and there, to no apparent purpose or function. Presumably it had all been brought up from the shop downstairs. I approached the television and knelt before it, careful to maintain a safe distance. Metal and mirrors, crystal and glass, and a few oily shapes that looked disturbingly organic. Up close, the stuff smelled . . . bad. Corrupt.

Bettie produced a camera from her embroidered purse and took a whole bunch of photos. She wanted to photograph me, too, and I let her. I was busy thinking. She finally ended up bending down beside me, sniffing disparagingly.

"Isn't this an absolutely awful place? There's underwear soaking in the bath, and no-one's cleaned up in here for months. Some men shouldn't be allowed to live on their own. You don't even want to know what I found in the toilet. This television is very impressive, though. Have you ever seen anything like it?"

"No," I said. "But then future and alien technology isn't my speciality. This could be genius, or it could be junk."

"Could it have enabled the television to look in on a broadcast from the Afterlife?"

"Who knows? But I wouldn't touch any of it, if I were you. It looks . . . unhealthy."

"Trust me, darling. I wouldn't touch *that* if it offered to buy me champagne."

I straightened up, and she straightened up with me. Her knees didn't creak. I looked round the apartment again. For all the clutter, the room was still basically characterless. No paintings or posters on the walls, no personal touches like photos or prized possessions, nothing to show Donavon had ever thought of this place as home. No; it was more like a place to stay while he was passing through on his way to better things. Once he got his lucky break . . . I was beginning to get an idea of who Pen Donavon might be, one of those desperate dreamers, always chasing that big break, that lucky find that would make him rich and famous and change his life forever. And maybe, this time he had . . .

I tried my gift again, hoping to pick up a ghost image of Pen Donavon's past, so I could follow it as he left . . . but once again the force from Outside slammed my inner eye shut the moment it started to open. I grimaced and shook my head slowly, waiting for the pain to settle. I was going to find out who was behind this, then do something about it. Something really nasty and violent.

"So, what do we do now?" said Bettie, who, despite everything I'd said, persisted on looking at me like I had all the answers.

"When faced with serious questions of a religious nature, there's only one place to go," I said. "And that is the Street of the Gods. If only because they always have the best gossip."

• • •

We took the Underground train. There are other ways of getting to the Street of the Gods, but the train is by far the safest. Bettie and I descended into the Underground system and strode through the cream-tiled tunnels covered in the usual graffiti, not all of it in human languages. CTHULHU DOES IT IN HIS SLEEP, was a new addition, along with THE EYES OF WALKER ARE UPON YOU. Bettie went to pay for our tickets, and I stopped her.

"It's all right, darling!" she said. "When you work for the *Unnatural Inquirer*, we pay for everything!"

"I don't pay," I said. I gestured at the ticket machine, and it opened obediently to let us pass. I smiled just a little smugly at Bettie. "Payment for an old case. One of the trains had gone rogue; people got on and then it wouldn't let them get off again. You could hear the trapped passengers beating helplessly on the walls, screaming for help."

"What happened?" said Bettie, her eyes wide. "What did you do?"

"I frightened the train," I said. "And it let everyone go."

"I shall never look at a train in the same way again," said Bettie.

We went down to the platform, giving the various buskers a wide berth. Especially the one singing four part harmonies with himself. It's one thing to drop a few coins in a hat, because the wheel turns for all of us, but it isn't always wise to listen to the music they play. Music really can have charms in the Nightside.

The platform was crowded, as usual. Half a dozen members of the Tribe of Gay Barbarians, standing around looking tough with their leathers and long swords, complete with shaved legs, pierced nipples, and heavy face make-up. A silverback gorilla wore an exquisitely cut formal suit, complete with top hat, cane, and a monocle screwed firmly into one eye. A Grey alien wearing fishnet stockings and suspenders, passing out tracts. And a very polite Chinese demon, sipping hot steaming blood from a thermos. The usual crowd.

The destination board offered the usual possibilities: SHADOWS FALL, HACELDAMA, STREET OF THE GODS. There are other destinations, other possibilities, but you have to go down into the deeper tunnels for those; and not everyone who goes down that far comes back up again.

A train roared in, right on time. A long, silvery bullet, preceded by a blast of approaching air that smelled of other places. The carriages were solid steel tubes, with only the heavily reinforced doors standing out. No windows. To get to its various destinations, the train had to travel through certain intervening dimensions; and none of them were the kinds of places where you'd want to see what was outside. The door hissed open, and Bettie and I stepped into the nearest carriage. The seats were green leather, and the steel walls were reassuringly thick and heavy. No-one else wanted to get into our carriage, despite the crowd on the platform.

The trip to the Street of the Gods was mostly uneventful. The few things that attacked us couldn't get in, and the dents in the steel walls had mostly smoothed themselves out again by the time the train pulled into the station. Bettie was still laughing and chattering as we made our way up the elevators to the Street of the Gods. You learn to take such things in your stride in the Nightside.

On the Street of the Gods, you can find a Church to pretty much anything that anyone has ever believed in. They stretched away forever, two long rows of organised worship, where the gods are always at home to callers. Prayers are heard here, and answered, so it pays to be careful what you say. You never know who might be listening. The most important Beings get the best spots, while everyone else fights it out for location in a Darwinian struggle for survival. Sometimes I think the whole Nightside runs on irony.

Most of the Beings on the Street of the Gods didn't want to talk to me. In fact, most of them hid inside their churches behind locked and bolted doors and refused to come out until I'd gone. Understandable; they were still rebuilding parts of the Street from the last time I'd been here. But there are always some determined to show those watching that they aren't afraid of anyone, so a few of the more up-and-coming Beings sauntered casually over to chat with me. A fairly ordinary-looking priest who said he was the newly risen Dagon. Stack! The Magnificient; a more or less humanoid alien who claimed to be slumming it from a higher dimension. And the Elegant Profundity, a guitar-carrying avatar from the Church of Clapton, who was so laid-back he was practically horizontal. The small and shifty God of Lost Things hung around, evasive as always. None of them professed to know anything about a broadcast from the Afterlife, let alone a DVD recording. Most of them were quite intrigued by the thought.

"It can't be authentic," said Dagon. "I mean, we're in the business of faith, not hard evidence. And if there had ever been a broadcast from the Hereafter, we'd have heard about it long before this."

"And just the idea of recording one is so . . . tacky," Stack! said, folding his four green arms across his sunken chest.

"But it could be very good for business," said the Elegant Profundity, strumming a minor chord on his Rickenbacker.

The group went very thoughtful.

"There's money to be made here," said Dagon. "Serious money. And there's nothing like business success to bring in bigger congregations. Everyone loves a winner."

"But . . . if this recording should prove real, and accurate, it would provide proof of What Comes After," Stack! said. "And the last thing anyone here wants is hard evidence of that. We derive our power from faith and worship. A true and actual Afterlife Recording could drive a lot of us out of business. Besides, most of Humanity isn't ready for the truth."

I regarded him thoughtfully. "Are you saying you know What Comes Next?"

Stack! squirmed uncomfortably, which given his rather fluid shape was a somewhat disturbing sight. "Well, no, not as such. I may be from a higher dimension, but not that high."

"You have to have faith," said the Elegant Profundity. "Solid evidence of the true nature of Heaven or Hell would only screw up everyone's life. It's one thing to suppose, quite another to know."

"This whole situation raises more questions than I'm comfortable with," I said. "What exactly is the DVD a recording of? Have there always been broadcasts from Heaven and Hell, and we never knew? And who were the broadcasts aimed at?"

"Each other?" said Bettie. "Maybe they just like to . . . keep in touch."

"But then why has no-one ever intercepted one of these broadcasts before?" I said. "Why should it suddenly turn up on someone's television set, no matter how much work's been done to it? And if anyone here so much as mentions moving in a mysterious way, I shall get cranky. Quite seriously and violently cranky."

"If there were such communications, on a regular basis, we would know about it," Dagon said firmly. "It's our job to provide mysteries and wonder, not grubby little facts."

"But what if it is true," Stack! said wistfully. "Was this interception of the broadcast a mistake, or deliberate? Are we supposed to know, at last? And who or what is behind it; and what could they hope to gain?"

"Money, probably," said the Elegant Profundity, and everyone nodded solemnly.

"Maybe we should all do our own DVDs," Stack! said.

"Can't risk falling behind . . . Let's face it, you can't have too much publicity."

"Sure," said the Elegant Profundity. "I've been releasing CDs on a regular basis ever since I got here. Rock and Roll Heaven won't build itself, you know."

"Yes, yes!" said Bettie Divine. "The *Unnatural Inquirer* could give away a new DVD every week, with the Sunday edition! Build your own collection!"

"We don't want the faithful sitting at home in front of their televisions," Dagon said firmly. "We want them here, in our Churches."

"We already sell religious statues, and reliquaries, and blessed artifacts," Stack! said reasonably. "DVDs are the future. For now. Does anyone here know about this Extra Definition thing?"

"New formats are the invention of the Devil," said the Elegant Profundity. "He's always been big on temptation. But people would pay through the nose for teachings direct from their God! And even second-hand faith is better than none."

"Royalty cheques outweigh collection plates any day," Stack! said. "I want you all to concentrate on one word: *franchise . . .*"

"Oh, come on!" said Dagon. "Where's that going to lead, the McChurch? You'll be talking about bringing in image consultants and focus groups next."

"Why not?" Stack! replied. "We have to move with the times. Faith is fine, but wealth lasts longer."

"Heretic!" said Dagon, and punched Stack! out with a very unpriestly left hook.

I took Bettie firmly by the arm, and we hurried away. Believers were coming running from all directions, eager to join the fray, and you really don't want to get caught in the middle of a religious war on the Street of the Gods. Especially not when the smiting starts. Someone always ends up throwing lightning bolts, and then it's bound to escalate. We headed back to the Underground station, discussing what we knew about previous attempts to communicate with the Other Side, so we wouldn't have to listen to the rising sounds of conflict and unpleasantness behind us.

It was already raining frogs.

"Surprisingly, Marconi is supposed to be the first man to use technology to try and make contact with the Hereafter," I said. "Some sources claim he only invented radio because he was trying to find a way to talk to his dead brother. There are even those who say he succeeded; though reports of what he heard are . . . disturbing."

"Then there are people who approach dying people in hospitals," said Bettie. "And persuade them to memorise messages from a bereaved family, to pass on to people already dead. There's usually money involved—to pay hospital bills or look after the dying person's family. The *Unnatural Inquirer* paid good money for a dozen messages to Elvis, but we never got a reply. What *was that*?"

"Don't look back," I said. "Then there are the Death-walkers. A disturbing bunch of action philosophers with a very hands-on approach to the Near Death Experience. They kill themselves, a necromancer holds them on the very brink for a while, and then he brings them back to life. The briefly departed are then questioned on what they saw, and who they spoke to, while they were dead. I've read some of the transcripts."

"And?"

"Either the dead lie a lot, or they have a really nasty sense of humour."

"I once did a piece on people who hear messages on radios trained to dead stations, or tape recorders left running in empty rooms," said Bettie. "I listened to a whole bunch of recordings, but I can't say I was convinced. It's all hiss and static, and something that might be voices, if you wanted it badly enough. It's like Rorschach ink-blots, where people see shapes that aren't really there. You hear what you want to hear. Was that a Church blowing up?"

"It's the pillars of salt that worry me," I said. "Just keep walking and talking."

"Then there's psychic imprinting," said Bettie, staring determinedly straight ahead. "You know, when a person stares at a blank piece of film and makes images appear. I did this marvellous piece on a man who could make naughty pictures appear on bathroom tiles, from two rooms away! The paper did a full colour supplement on most of them. You could only get the full set by mail order, under plain cover."

"Psychic imprinting is more common than most people like to think," I said. "That's where most ghost images come from. And genius loci, where bad things happening poisons the surroundings, to produce Bad Places. Like Fun Faire."

"Wait just a minute, darling," said Bettie. "I heard about what just happened there! Was that you?"

I simply smiled.

"Oh, poo! You're no fun at all sometimes."

"That augmented television set bothers me," I said. "Could Pen Donavon have accidentally invented something that allowed him to Listen In, however briefly, on something Humanity was never supposed to know about? Stranger things have happened, and most of them right here in the Nightside. This place has always attracted rogue scientists and very free thinkers, come here in pursuit of the kinds of knowledge and practices that are banned everywhere else, and quite properly, too. Walker has a whole group of his people dedicated to tracking these idiots, then shutting them down, with extreme prejudice if necessary. Unless what they're doing looks to be unusually interesting, or profitable, in which case their work gets confiscated for the greater good. Which means the scientists get to work exclusively for the Authorities, somewhere very secure, for the rest of their lives."

"Except there aren't any Authorities, any more," said Bettie. "So who do these scientists work for now?"

"Good question," I said. "If you ever find out . . ."

"You'll read about it in the *Unnatural Inquirer*." Bettie smiled cheerfully. "I love the way you talk about these things so casually. I only get to hear about stuff like this at second or third remove, and there's rarely any proof. You're right there in the thick of things. Must be such fun . . ."

"Not always the word I'd use," I said. "And you are not to quote me. I don't care what you print, but Walker might. And he'd be more likely to come after you than me."

"Let him," Bettie said airily. "The *Unnatural Inquirer* looks after its own. John, you're frowning. Why are you frowning? Should we start running?"

"If Pen Donavon had found a way to Listen In and got noticed," I said slowly, "he might have attracted the attention of Heaven or Hell. Which is rarely a good thing. They might send agents to silence him, and destroy the Recording."

"Oh, dear," said Bettie. "Are we talking angels? The Nightside's still putting itself back together after the last angel war."

"I wish people would stop looking at me like the angel war was all my fault," I said.

"Well, it was; wasn't it?"

"Not as such, no!"

"You can be such a disappointment, sometimes," said Bettie Divine.

# FOUR

*When Collectors Go Bad*

Back in the Nightside proper, I headed for Uptown, that relatively refined area where the better class of establishments and members-only clubs gather together and circle the wagons, to keep out the riff-raff. People like me, and anyone I might know. I had a particular destination in mind, but I didn't tell Bettie. Some subjects need to be sneaked up on, approached slowly and cautiously, so as not to freak out the easily upset. Bettie clearly thought she'd been around and seen it all, but there are some people and places that would make a snot demon puke, on general principles.

"Where exactly are we going?" said Bettie, looking eagerly about her.

"Well," I said, "when you're on the trail of something rare and unique, the place to start is with the Collector. He's spent the best part of his life in pursuit of the extraordinary and the uncommon, often by disreputable, underhanded, and downright dishonest means. He's a thief and a grave-robber, a despoiler of archaeological sites, and no museum or private cabinet of curiosities is safe from him. He's even got his own collection of weird time machines, so he can loot and ransack the Past of all its choicest items. If there's a gap in history where something important ought to be, you can bet the Collector's been there. He's bound to have heard about the Afterlife Recording by now, and, faced with the prospect of such a singular and significant item, you can bet he won't rest till he's tracked it down."

Bettie looked actually awe-struck. "The Collector . . . Oh, wow. The paper's been trying to get an interview with him for years. Mind you, half the people you talk to swear he's nothing more than an urban myth, something historians use to frighten their children. But you know him personally! That is so cool! Has he really got the Holy Grail? The Spear of Destiny? The Maltese Falcon?"

"Given the sheer size of his collection, anything's possible," I said. "Except maybe that last one."

"There are those who say the two of you have a history," Bettie said guilelessly.

"If you're fishing in your pocket for your mini tape recorder, forget it," I said pleasantly. "I lifted it off you before we even left the *Unnatural Inquirer* offices. I don't do *on the record*."

"Oh, poo," said Bettie. And then she smiled dazzlingly. "Doesn't matter. I have a quite remarkable memory. And what I can't remember, I'll make up. So, tell me all about the Collector. How did you meet?"

"He was an old friend of my father's," I said.

Bettie frowned. "But . . . some of the stories say he's your mortal enemy?"

"That, too," I said. "That's the Nightside for you."

"Where's he based these days?" Bettie said casually.

I grinned. "That really would be a scoop for you, wouldn't it? Unfortunately, I have no idea, at present. He used to store his collection in a secret base up on the Moon, sunk deep under the Sea of Tranquility, but he moved it after I . . . dropped in, for a little visit."

"Couldn't you have used your gift to find it again?"

"The Collector is seriously protected. By Forces and Powers even I would think twice about messing with."

"Still . . . you've actually seen his collection! How cool is that? What did you see? What has he got? *Did you take any photos?*"

I smiled. "I never betray a confidence."

"But he's your mortal enemy!"

"Not always," I said. "It's . . . complicated."

Bettie shrugged easily and slipped her arm through mine. My first impulse was to pull away, but I didn't. Her arm felt good where it was. I looked at her thoughtfully, but she'd given up on grilling me for the moment and was looking interestedly about her.

"I don't think I've ever been this deep into Uptown. You don't come here unless you are almost obscenely wealthy. I'll bet there are shops here where a pair of shoes would cost more than my annual salary. Remind me to steal a pair before we leave. Where are we going, exactly?"

"I need to talk to Walker," I said.

Bettie slammed to a halt, stopping me with her. "The head man himself? Darling, you don't mess around, do you?"

"If anyone knows where the Collector hangs his hat these days, it'll be Walker," I said. "Can we start moving again?"

She nodded stiffly, and we set off at a somewhat slower pace than before.

"But, gosh, I mean . . . *Walker*," said Bettie, giving me her wide-eyed look again. "Our very own polite and civilised and extremely dangerous lord and master? The man who can make people disappear if he doesn't like the look of them? That Walker? There is a definite limit as to how far I'm prepared to go for this story, and annoying Walker is right there at the top of my list of Things Not To Do."

"You'll be fine, as long as you're with me." I tried hard to sound calm and confident. "He'll talk to me. Partly because Walker is another old friend of my father's. Partly because he's an old friend of the Collector. But mostly because I shall dazzle him with my charming personality."

"Maybe I'll stay outside while you talk to him," said Bettie.

I grinned at her and noticed abruptly that she wasn't wearing her polka-dot dress any more. She was now wearing a creamy off-the-shoulder number, very chic, and a pink pill-box hat with a veil. The horns on her forehead peeked demurely out from under the brim of the hat, lifting the veil just a little. I decided not to say anything.

"Is this really such a good idea, sweetie?" Bettie said finally. "I mean, *Walker* . . . That man is seriously scary. He's disappeared at least nine of the *Unnatural Inquirer's* reporters because they were getting too close to something he didn't want known. Or at least discussed. We know it was him, because he sent us personally signed *In Deep Condolence* cards."

"Yeah," I said. "That sounds like Walker."

"I don't want to be disappeared, John! It would be very bad for my career. Promise me you'll protect me. I am too young, too talented, and too utterly gorgeous in a fashionably understated way to be disappeared! It would be a crime against journalism."

"Relax," I said. "You'll be fine. I can handle Walker."

I don't like to lie to people, unless I have to, but sometimes you have to say what people want to hear to get them to do what you want them to do. And I had to talk to Walker. He was the only one who might know where the Collector was hiding out these days, who might be willing to tell me. It was always a calculated risk, talking to Walker. In the end, when we finally run out of excuses, one of us is going to kill the other. I've always known that. And so has he.

We like each other. We've saved each other's lives. It's complicated. It's the Nightside.

"Do you need your gift to find Walker?" Bettie asked, staring distractedly about her as though half-expecting him to suddenly appear out of some door or side alley, just from the mention of his name.

"No," I said. "I know where he'll be. Where he always is at this time. Taking tea at his Gentleman's Club."

"Walker belongs to a club?" said Bettie. "Result, darling! A definite exclusive! Which club?"

"There is only one club for those of Walker's exalted position," I said. "The oldest and most exclusive club in the Nightside. The Londinium Club."

Bettie looked sharply at me. "But . . . that was destroyed. During the Lilith War. We published photos. That was where the Authorities were killed. And eaten."

"Quite right," I said. "But it's back. Word is, the Club rebuilt itself. Any building that's survived everything the Nightside can throw at it for over two thousand years isn't going to let a little thing like being destroyed in a war slow it down."

"Oh," said Bettie. "Do you mind that I'm holding your arm?"

"No," I said. "I don't mind."

• • •

The last time I'd seen the Londinium Club, during the height of the Lilith War, it had been one hell of a mess. The magnificent Roman façade had been cracked and holed, smoke-blackened and fire-damaged. The great marble steps leading up to the single massive door had been fouled with blood and shit. And the Club's legendary Doorman, who had kept out the uninvited and unwelcome for centuries beyond counting, had been torn apart, his severed head impaled on the railings. Inside, it had been even worse.

But now everything seemed back to normal, right down to the fully restored Roman façade. Which I'd always found rather crude, to be honest. There was a new Doorman, however. It seemed the Club could only restore itself, and not those who'd died defending it. Just as well, really. A lot of the Club's members were no loss to anyone, for all their wealth and power. Anyone rich and powerful enough to belong to the Londinium Club had almost certainly done appalling and unspeakable things to get there. And that very definitely included Walker.

The new Doorman was a tall and elegantly slender fellow dressed in the full finery of Regency fashion. Right down to the heart-shaped beauty mark on his cheek, the poser. He moved deliberately forward to block my way as I started up the steps towards the door. I stopped right in front of him and eased my arm out of Bettie's so I could give the Doorman my full attention. He looked down his nose at me, and there was a lot of it to look down. His eyes were cold and distant, and his thin smile was carefully calculated to be polite without containing the slightest trace of warmth or welcome. I was sure Bettie was giving him her brightest smile, but the Doorman and I only had eyes for each other.

"I have the name and face of every current Member of the Londinium Club committed to memory, sir," said the Doorman. He made the *sir* sound like an insult. "And I believe I am correct in saying that you, sir, and this . . . person, are not Members in good standing. Therefore, you have no business being here."

"Wrong," I said. "I'm here to see Walker."

"He does not wish to be seen, sir. And particularly not by the likes of you. You may leave now."

"I don't think so," I said. "Being faced down by a little snot like you would be bad for my reputation. One last chance—go and tell Walker I'm here."

"Leave," said the Doorman. "You are not welcome here. You will never be welcome here."

"Just once, I'd love to do this the easy way," I said wistfully. "Now step aside, fart face, or I'll do something amusing to you."

The Doorman sniffed disdainfully, gestured languidly with one hand, and a shimmering wall of force sprang up between us. I fell back a step, sensing the terrible power running through the field. This was new. The old Doorman had relied on sheer obnoxious personality, of which he had a lot, to keep the riff-raff out. That, and a punch that could concuss a cow. Presumably the Club had decided it needed a more sturdy defence these days. The new Doorman wasn't actually sneering at me, he wouldn't lower himself that much; but it felt like he was. And I couldn't have that.

I stepped forward again, so close to the field I could feel it prickling on my skin, and looked the Doorman right in the eye. He met my gaze coldly, with a supercilious stare. I kept looking at him, and he began to shake, as he realised he couldn't look away. Beads of sweat popped out all over his face as I held his gaze with mine, and he started to make low, whimpering sounds.

"Drop the screen," I said. "We're coming in."

The screen snapped off. I looked away, and the Doorman collapsed, sitting down suddenly on the steps as though all the strength had gone out of his legs. He actually flinched back as I led Bettie up the steps past him. She looked at me, frowning, as we approached the massive front door of the Londinium Club.

"What the hell did you do to him?"

"I stared him down," I said.

"That really wasn't a very nice thing to do, sweetie. He was only doing his job. I'm not sure I want you holding my arm any more."

"Suit yourself," I said. "I don't always have time for nice. Or the inclination."

"You're full of surprises, aren't you?"

"You have no idea," I said.

The huge door swung open before us. Just as well; I'd had something particularly unpleasant and destructive in mind in case it hadn't. Inside, the main foyer was exactly as I remembered it, intimidatingly large, unbearably stuffy, and smotheringly luxurious. Mosaics and paintings and marble pillars, and a general air of smug exclusivity. The last time I'd been here there'd been blood and bodies everywhere, but you'd never know it now. Wars came and apocalypses went, but the Londinium Club goes on forever.

Some say there are terrible caverns deep beneath the Club, where the oldest Members still gather to worship something ancient and awful. Baphomet, some say, or the King in Yellow, or the Serpent in the Sun. But there are always rumours like that in the Nightside.

A few people passed us, looking very prosperous and important. They studiously ignored me, and Bettie. I caught the eye of a liveried footman, and he came reluctantly over to see what I wanted.

"You've been here before," said Bettie, her voice hushed for once by the sheer presence of the place.

"I've been everywhere before," I said. "Mind you, I've also been thrown out of practically everywhere, at one time or another."

"I've never seen anything like this . . ."

"Don't let it get to you. For all the Club's opulence, you couldn't spit in the dining-room without being sure of hitting at least one complete scumbag."

She giggled suddenly and put one hand to her mouth. The footman came to a halt before me and bowed politely. Since I was in the Club, I obviously belonged there. His was not to question why, no matter how much he might want to. He'd bowed to worse, in his time. He managed to imply all this without actually saying a word. It was a remarkable performance. I felt like applauding.

"Walker," I said.

"In the main dining-room, sir. Dining, with guests. Should I announce you, sir?"

"And spoil the surprise?" I said. "Heaven forfend. You run along. We can look after ourselves."

The footman backed away at speed, not even waiting for a tip. Which was just as well, really. I headed casually for the main dining area, with Bettie tagging along at my side like an over-excited puppy. No-one challenged us. It's all about attitude. You can get away with murder if you look like you belong.

I pushed open the dining-room door, stepped inside, then stopped right there, pushing Bettie slightly to one side so that we were concealed from the crowded room by a fortuitously placed potted aspidistra. I hushed her before she could say anything and peered between the leaves. All the tables were full, mostly occupied by large sturdy types in formal suits, eating basic stodgy food because it reminded them of the good old days of school dinners. None of them looked at each other. They were there for peace and quiet, not to socialise.

Walker had to be the exception, of course. He was currently holding court with some of the more august personages jockeying for position to take the place of the recently deceased Authorities. They sat stiffly in stiff-backed chairs, nursing expensive liqueurs and oversized cigars and talking loudly to show they didn't give a damn who overheard them. They smiled and nodded and were polite enough, and you'd never know they were deadly rivals who'd happily slaughter each other at the first sign of weakness. This was politics, after all, and there were rules of etiquette to follow. Yesterday's enemy might be tomorrow's friend, or at least ally.

"Hush," I said quietly to Bettie. "Watch and listen. You might learn something interesting. You know who those people are, with Walker?"

"Of course," she said, putting her mouth so close to my ear I could feel her breath on the side of my face. "Walker's the smart city gent. The older gentleman to his left in the military uniform is General Condor. The revolting specimen to Walker's right is Uptown Taffy Lewis. And the woman sitting opposite Walker is Queen Helena, ex-Monarch of the Ice Kingdoms."

"Very good," I said. "Now let's see if you read anything more than the gossip columns. What can you tell me about Walker's guests?"

Bettie smiled, glad of a chance to show off her reporter's expertise. "General Condor comes from a future time-line. Arrived here through a Timeslip and got stranded in the Nightside when it closed. Word is he used to be in charge of some kind of Space Fleet, star-ships and the like, keeping the peace in some future Empire or Federation. He was leading the troops into battle against some kind of Rebellion, when his flagship came under fire and was blown apart. He only escaped at the last moment in a life-boat." She laughed briefly. "He doesn't approve of us. A very upright and moral man, is our General. Since he arrived here he'd made it his business to first support, and then lead, all the right causes. He wants to reform us and save our souls, the poor fool. The *Unnatural Inquirer*'s been trying to dig up some dirt on him for ages, but unfortunately it seems he really is as worthy and boring as he claims."

I nodded, looking the General over. Condor was a tall, straight-backed military type, in a surprisingly old-fashioned bottle-green uniform, complete with peaked cap. Even sitting down, he looked like he was still at attention. His face was deeply lined, scarred here and there, but his blue eyes were cold and piercing under bushy white eyebrows. He had to be in late middle age, but there didn't look to be an ounce of give in him.

I'd run into him a few times, here and there. He didn't approve of me, or people like me, but then it would be hard to find anyone or anything he did approve of in the Nightside. Our free trade in vice and depravity and damnation appalled him. A good man, perhaps, and no doubt brave enough standing on the poop-deck of his star-ship, facing terrible odds; but his stark black-and-white philosophy had no place in the Nightside. On the one hand, he was desperate to return to his own time and his own people, and take up the battle again, but on the other he was realistic enough to know he might never get back. And so he had decided to take on the Nightside, as a challenge. As an evil to be overcome. He now led, or at least represented, all those various interests inside the Nightside who wanted to clean the place up, for their own philosophical, financial, or political reasons.

General Condor liked to talk about redemption, and potential, and all the things we might achieve, if only we could control our darker urges and learn to work together. He couldn't seem to understand that people only came here to indulge their darker urges. He was a good man, in the wrong place. And the Nightside does so love to break a hero.

"How about the slug in the ill-fitting dress jacket?" I said.

"Easy. Everyone knows Uptown Taffy Lewis," said Bettie. She made brief retching noises. "He owns most of the prime real estate in the Nightside, now the Griffin is finally dead and gone. He has enormous economic leverage and isn't shy about using it to get his own way. Word is he can't get any richer, so now he wants power. He maintains his own private army of bully-boys, enforcers, and leg-breakers, and anyone who speaks out against Taffy tends to find out why terribly quickly. He wants to be the new Griffin, the new king of the castle, and have us all bow down to him. He has pretensions to style and elegance and gentility, but wouldn't recognise them if he fell over them in the gutter. The man was born a cheap thug, and he'll never change. The *Inquirer*'s run any number of exposés on him and said all kinds of nasty things, but he's rich enough that he doesn't care. Hateful man. They say he ate his brother."

"Completely accurate," I said.

Uptown Taffy Lewis was a large man, in all the wrong ways. The expertly cut suit couldn't conceal his many rolls of fat, any more than his current polite expression could hide his cold piggy eyes or cruel mouth. Taffy didn't just want to be big man at the trough, he wanted to keep everyone else out, simply because he could. Own it all, control it all, and have the power to destroy it all. And then use that power to make everyone else beg for the scraps from his table. Probably had a really small penis. Uptown Taffy Lewis wanted the Nightside because it was there.

He'd tried to have me killed on several occasions. I didn't take it personally. For Taffy, it was always just business.

"And ex-Queen Helena?" I said to Bettie.

"Nasty piece of work, by all accounts." Bettie curled her perfect upper lip. "Powerful, talented, and dangerous in all sorts of unpleasant ways, though it's hard to say whether her power derives from science or sorcery. She can kill with a look or a touch, and they say she can enslave a man by whispering his name. The official word is that she arrived here via a Timeslip from some far future time-line, where the sun is going out and the ice covers everything. A cold woman from a cold world. But you can take that with as many grains of salt as you like; people who turn up through Timeslips tell all sorts of tales, and there's rarely any way of checking. She claims to have been the Queen of the whole world, and she has the way of royalty about her, but . . . Odd that a Queen should be travelling alone, don't you think? Anyway, she's certainly single-minded enough about becoming royalty again, either back in her own time or right here in the Nightside. She has a lot of followers here; people who like to think they know a real monarch when they see one. She's been selling titles to anyone who can raise the money."

I nodded. I knew the type. (Ex-)Queen Helena was a disturbing sight. Tall, regal, haughty, and more impressive than God, she sat on her chair as though it was a throne fashioned from the bones of her enemies. She wore thick white furs, a diamond tiara, and her long flat hair was so blonde as to be practically colourless. Her deathly pale skin was tinged with blue, and her face and bare arms were covered with intricate patterns of painted-on circuitry. There were subtle bulges here and there under her skin, suggesting concealed high-tech implants. They raised and lowered themselves, apparently according to her moods.

"Well done, Bettie," I said. "Very accurate descriptions, nicely succinct and more than usually informed. There are investigative journalists on the *Night Times* who wouldn't have been able to tell me that much. You're not just a pretty face, are you?"

She smiled easily. "I was wondering how long the wide-eyed act would fool you. You don't get to be one of the *Unnatural Inquirer*'s top reporters by batting your eyes and simpering at people. Though you'd be surprised how far that can get you, even with important people. Men are such simple, basic creatures, bless them. For the others, it's amazing how many weak spots and vulnerabilities good research can turn up. I smile, I watch, I listen, I draw conclusions, and I write it all up afterwards. You weren't fooled by the act for one minute, were you?"

"It's a good act," I said, generously. "Now hush and observe Walker at work. See how he influences and manipulates people, without them even realising."

"Things have got to change," General Condor was saying heavily. He leaned forward across the table to glare at Walker, who seemed entirely unperturbed. The General's voice was slow and deliberate, used to giving orders and having them obeyed. He had the air of a man people would follow: bluff, experienced, sure, and certain. A man who knew what he was doing. He jabbed a heavy finger in Walker's face. "The Nightside can't continue as it has—a haven for all human depravity and weakness. It'll tear itself apart with the Griffin and the Authorities gone. The signs are clear for everyone to see, first the angel war, and then the Lilith War . . . Left to its own devices, the Nightside will inevitably tear itself apart."

"There have always been wars, and destruction, and changes at the top," Walker said calmly. "But the Nightside goes on. It has survived for thousands of years, and I see no reason why it shouldn't continue as it is for thousands more. The world has always had a taste for freak shows."

General Condor scowled. "That might have been true while the Authorities were running things and supporting the Nightside in the same way a farmer looks after the goose that lays golden eggs; but they're gone now. Along with their blinkered preoccupation with trade and profit. It's time for someone to take the longer view and make the Nightside into something better."

"Nothing wrong with making money," Uptown Taffy Lewis said immediately. His voice was soft and breathy, his great chest and belly rising and falling as though every breath cost him something. "The Nightside exists to provide people with the pleasures and pursuits they can't get anywhere else. The things civilised people aren't supposed to want, but do anyway. And they'll pay through the nose for it, every time. Keep your rigid morality to yourself, General. We don't need simple-minded do-gooders coming in from outside and meddling with a system that's worked fine for thousands of years."

"The man has a point, General," said Walker. "It's hard to argue with success."

"All the things I've seen here," said the General, "the marvels and wonders, the amazing achievements, the incredible possibilities . . . If you would only work together instead of cutting each other's throats over a penny's profits, the things you could do . . . The Nightside could become the pinnacle of human civilisation! Instead of the moral cesspit it is now. You could all be gods if you'd only throw off the chains that hold you back!"

"Not everyone wants to be a god," said Walker. "In fact, I'd say we already have far too many. I've been thinking about ordering a cull . . . Too many Chiefs only confuse the Indians. Wouldn't you agree, Helena?"

"You may address me as Queen Helena, or Your Majesty," she said immediately, her voice suitably chilly. The other two looked at her sharply. You didn't talk that way to Walker if you liked breathing, and having your bones stay where they were. But he nodded thoughtfully to Queen Helena, and she continued.

"People must know their place. For many, it is their nature to be ruled. To have someone ready to make the important decisions for them. I am not a lone voice in this. I speak for others such as I in the Nightside."

"The Exiles," said Walker. "All the other kings and queens and emperors who wound up here, via Timeslips or other unfortunate accidents. So many that there seems to be something of a glut of rulers on the market, at the moment."

"People of power and prestige," Queen Helena said firmly. "People who do not care for the way things are. The Nightside needs to be taken in hand and ruled by people suited to the task."

"Would you agree with that, Taffy?" said Walker.

"No-one tells me what to do," said Uptown Taffy Lewis. He almost sounded amused. "No-one rules the Nightside. Never has, never will. We make our own way. This is the last truly free place left on Earth, where everything and anything is possible. Even the Authorities knew enough to keep their distance. Right, Walker? I represent people, too. I speak for the businesspeople of the

Nightside, and we will not stand by and see our rights trampled on." He glared at Helena, and then at General Condor. "You don't belong here, either of you. We like the Nightside just the way it is; and neither of you have the support or the power to change anything that matters. I own most of the land the Nightside stands on; my associates own most of the rest. We can bankrupt anyone who doesn't back us up. And we can raise armies, if necessary, to defend what is ours."

"I have led armies," said General Condor. "There's more to it than giving orders."

"I have led armies, too," said Queen Helena. Something in her voice made the others look at her. She smiled coldly. "I did not come here by accident. No arbitrary Timeslip brought me here; I can go home anytime I want. To the ancient and melancholy Ice Kingdoms, where my armies wait for me. It has been a long time since the Armies of the Evening have had a cause worth fighting for. Because we killed everyone else who stood against us, in the long twilight of Earth. I have no wish to be Queen of an empty world. Not when I can bring my armies here and make the Nightside my own."

General Condor and Uptown Taffy Lewis looked at her, then at each other, and finally at Walker, who smiled easily.

"Why risk your armies, and your life, to secure a city, when you already have a world of your own?"

Queen Helena smiled back at him coldly, her blue-tinged lips drawing back to reveal perfect sharp teeth. "I like it here. It's warm."

"Ice melts when the going gets hot," said Taffy.

"You dare?" Queen Helena stood up, glaring down at them all. Strange metallic shapes surfaced in the blue-white flesh of her arms. Silver-grey barrels targeted Taffy and the General.

*"That's enough!"* Walker didn't stand up. He didn't need to. He was using the Voice. *"Put your weapons away, Helena."*

The Queen of the Evening shook and shuddered, her lips drawing back in a frustrated grimace, as she fought the Voice and failed. The implanted technology sank back into her arms, bluish skin closing seamlessly over it. She snarled furiously at Walker, a fierce, animal sound, then she turned abruptly and stalked away. Servants hurried to get out of her way. General Condor and Uptown Taffy Lewis rose to their feet, bowed stiffly to Walker, and then they left, too, careful to maintain a respectful distance between them. Perhaps they were worried Walker would use the Voice on them. He watched them go thoughtfully, and then turned unhurriedly in his chair and looked right at me.

"I'll see you now, Taylor."

I nodded and smiled, and moved unhurriedly forward to join him at his table. Bettie stuck close to my side.

"How did he know we were there?" she whispered.

"He's Walker," I said.

Bettie and I sat down in the newly vacated seats, facing

Walker. He looked perfectly calm and at ease in his elegant city suit, his public school tie neatly tied in a Windsor knot. He didn't seem particularly pleased to see me, but then he rarely did.

"Nicely played," I said. "You set them at each other's throats without once having to make clear your own position. It's always good to see a real professional at work."

Walker smiled briefly and turned his attention to Bettie. "I see we have a representative of the Press with us. And a more charming example than most. I feel I should warn you that recording devices won't function inside the Club. And I am very definitely not available for an interview. I've read some of your work, Miss Divine. You show promise. I'm sure you'll make a name for yourself once you get a job at a real newspaper."

Bettie smiled widely, almost overwhelmed that Walker had heard of her and was familiar with her work. I could have told her; Walker knows everyone.

"Looks like the vultures are gathering over the Nightside," I said. "Would I be right in thinking that people are being encouraged to choose sides? Whether they want to or not?"

"Which side would you be on, Taylor, if push came to shove?" said Walker.

"My side," I said.

Walker nodded slightly. And perhaps it was only my imagination that he looked a little disappointed in me.

"You've heard about the Afterlife Recording?" I said.

"Of course you have. It's gone missing, and I've been hired to find it."

"Then find it quickly," said Walker. "Before forces from Above or Below decide to get involved. The last time that happened was a disaster for all of us."

"I wish everyone would stop looking at me like the angel war was all my fault!"

"It was," said Walker.

"Can I quote you?" said Bettie.

"No," said Walker. "What do you want from me, Taylor?"

"I want to know where the Collector is hiding out these days," I said. "If anyone knows anything about the Afterlife Recording, it will be him. That's if he hasn't already got his fat sweaty hands on it, of course."

"Of course," said Walker. "Mark never could resist the challenge of the chase . . . Very well. The Collector is currently hiding his collection inside another collection. To be exact, inside the Museum of Unnatural History."

"An exclusive!" said Bettie, beaming happily.

"Not for long," said Walker. "He'll move again once he's been found. Poor Mark."

"You know the Collector personally?" said Bettie. "Is that how you know where he's been hiding?"

"I know where everyone is," said Walker. "That's my job."

"Do you know where the offices of the *Unnatural Inquirer* are located?"

"Yes."

"Ah," said Bettie Divine. "Then I'd better contact the Sub-Editor and tell him to tone down tomorrow's editorial."

"I would," said Walker. He looked back at me. "I can't speak for what kind of reception you can expect from Mark. The three of us might have worked together to end the Lilith War, but you can't rely on that to mean anything. His collection is all that really matters to him these days. He's come a long way from the man I and your father once knew. Don't turn your back on him."

I considered the point. "Can I say you sent me?"

Walker shrugged. "If you think it'll do any good. Find the Recording, John. And then, if you've got any sense, destroy it."

"The *Unnatural Inquirer* owns exclusive rights to the Afterlife Recording!" Bettie said immediately.

"There is that," said Walker. "Certainly I couldn't think of a better way to discredit it."

Bettie started to say something else, but I took her firmly by the elbow, levered her up out of her chair, nodded quickly to Walker and moved her off towards the door. She made a show of fighting me, but I could tell she was glad of a way to leave Walker without losing face.

"The way you and he talked," she said, as we walked across the lobby. "You two are close, aren't you? I never knew that. I don't think anyone does . . . There's a lot going on there that you're not telling me."

"Of course," I said. "I'm protecting you."

"From what?"

"From never being able to sleep again."

• • •

We left the Londinium Club, and strolled unhurriedly through the sleazy streets of the Nightside. Amber light from the street-lamps was easily shouldered aside by the fierce electric colours of the flashing neon signs, and the grubby pavements were crowded with preoccupied, anxious figures, all intent on their own private dreams and damnations. Sweet sounds and madder music blasted out of the open doors of clubs where the fun never stopped, and you could dance till you dropped. Brazen windows showed off all the latest temptations, barkers boasted of the attractions to be found inside for the discerning patron, and sin went walking openly down the street in the very latest fuck-me shoes.

The traffic roared past, never slowing, never stopping, because it wasn't there for us.

Visiting the Londinium Club's dining-room had made me peckish, so I stopped at a concession stand and treated Bettie and me to something wriggling on a stick. The meat was sharp and spicy, and just a bit crunchy.

"Would I regret it if I was to ask exactly what this is that I'm eating?" said Bettie, as we continued down the street.

"Almost certainly," I said cheerfully.

"Then I won't ask. Am I supposed to eat the head, too?"

"If you want."

"But it's looking at me!"

"Then eat it from the other end."

"You really know how to show a girl a good time, Taylor."

We walked a while in silence, chewing thoughtfully.

"I've never been to the Museum of Unnatural History," Bettie said finally. "I always meant to go and take a look at what they've got there. I understand they have some really interesting exhibits. But it's not really me. I don't do the educational thing."

"They've got a *Tyrannosaurus rex*," I said.

Bettie threw away her stick and looked at me. "What, the complete skeleton?"

"No, in a cage."

Her eyes widened. "Wow; a real *T. rex*! I wonder what they feed it . . ."

"People who litter, probably."

The Museum of Unnatural History is very modern-looking. The French may have a glass pyramid outside the Louvre, but we have a glass tesseract. An expanded cube that exists in four spatial dimensions. A bit hard on the eyes, but a small price to pay for style. The tesseract isn't merely the entrance to the Museum, it contains the whole thing inside its own very private and secure pocket dimension. The Museum needs a whole dimension to itself, to contain all the wonders and marvels it has accumulated down the years; from the Past, the Present, and any number of Future time-lines.

I walked steadily forward into the glass tesseract,

Bettie clinging firmly to my arm again, and almost immediately we were standing in the Museum's entrance lobby. I say almost immediately; there was a brief sensation of falling, of alien voices howling all around, and a huge eye turning slowly to look in our direction . . . but you tend to take things like that in your stride in the Nightside. The lobby itself was quaintly and pleasantly old-fashioned. All polished oak and brass and Victorian fittings, marble floors with built-in mosaics, and any number of wire stands packed with books and pamphlets and learned volumes on sale, inspired by the many famous (or currently fashionable) exhibits. Once again the ticket barrier opened itself for me, and Bettie looked at me, impressed.

"This is even better than having an expense account. Did you do something important for the Museum, too?"

"No," I said. "I think they're just scared of me."

The uniformed staff were all Neanderthals—big and muscular, with hairy hands, low brows, and chinless jaws filled with large blocky teeth. The deep-set eyes were kind, but distant. Neanderthals performed all the menial work in the Museum, in return for not being exhibits. They were also in charge of basic security, and rumour had it they were allowed to eat anyone they caught. I asked one to take us to the Director of the Museum, and he hooted softly before beckoning us to follow him. He had a piercing in one ear, and a badge on his lapel saying UNIONISE NOW!

He led us deep into the Museum, and Bettie's head

swung back and forth, trying to take in everything at once. I was almost as bad. The Museum really does have something for everyone. A miniature blue whale, presented in a match-box, to give it some scale. I wondered vaguely how it would taste on toast. More disturbingly, half of one wall was taken up with a Victorian display of stuffed and mounted wee winged fairies, pinned through the abdomen. Only a few inches tall, the fairies were perfectly formed, their stretched-out wings glued in place and showing off all the delicate colours of a soap bubble. They had many-faceted insect eyes, and vicious barbed stingers hung down between their toothpick legs. In the next room there were tall glass jars containing fire-flies and iceflies, mermaids with monkey faces, and a display of alien genitalia through the ages. Bettie got the giggles.

On a somewhat larger scale, one whole room was taken up with a single great diorama featuring the fabled last battle between Man and Elf. The dozens of full-sized figures were very impressive. The Men, in their spiked and greaved armour, looked brave and heroic, while the Fae looked twisted and evil. Which was pretty much the way it was, by all accounts. There was a lot of blood and gore and severed limbs, but I suppose you need that these days to bring in the tourists. Another huge diorama showed a pack of werewolves on the prowl, under a full moon. Each figure showed a different stage of the transformation, from man to wolf. They all looked unnervingly real; but up close there was a definite smell of sawdust and preservatives.

Another group of figures showed a pack of ghouls, teaching a human changeling child how to feed as they did. The Museum of Unnatural History presented such things without comment. History is what it is and not what we would have it be.

There were a fair number of people around, but the place wasn't what you'd call crowded, despite all the wonders and treasures on display. People don't tend to come to the Nightside for such intellectual pleasures. And tourism's been right down since the recent wars. The Museum is said to be heavily subsidised, but I couldn't tell you who by. Most of the exhibits are donated; the Museum certainly didn't have the budget to buy them.

The uniformed Neanderthal finally brought us to the Museum's current pride and joy, the *Tyrannosaurus rex*. The cage they'd made to hold it was huge, a good three hundred feet in diameter and a hundred feet high. The bars were reinforced steel, but the cage's interior had been made over into a reconstruction of the *T. rex*'s time, to make it feel at home. The cage contained a primordial jungle, with vast trees and luxurious vegetation, under a blazing sun. The illusion was perfect. The terrible heat didn't pass beyond the bars, but a gusting breeze carried out the thick and heavy scents of crushed vegetation, rotting carrion, and even the damp smells of a nearby salt flat. I could even hear the buzzing of oversized flies and other insects. The trees were tall and dark, with drooping serrated leaves, and what ground I could see was mostly mud, stamped flat.

But it was all dominated by the tyrant king himself, *Tyrannosaurus rex*. It towered above us, almost as tall as the trees, much bigger than I'd expected. It stood very still, half-hidden amongst the shadows of rotting vegetation, watching us through the bars. There was a definite sense of weight and impact about it, as though the ground itself would shake and shudder when it moved. Its scales were a dull grey-green, splashed here and there with the dried blood of recent kills. It panted loudly through its open mouth, revealing jagged teeth like a shark's. The small gripping arms high up on the chest didn't seem ridiculous at all, when seen full size. I had no doubt they could tear me apart in a moment. But it was the eyes that troubled me the most; set far back in the ugly wedge-shaped head, they were sharp and knowing . . . and they hated. They looked right at me, and they knew me. This was no mere animal, no simple savage beast. It knew it was a prisoner, and it knew who was responsible; and it lived for the moment when it would inevitably break free and take a terrible revenge.

"How the hell did they get hold of a *T. rex*?" said Bettie, her voice unconsciously hushed.

"You should read your own paper more often," I said. "There was a sudden invasion of dinosaurs through a Timeslip, earlier this year. Some fifty assorted beasts got through, before Walker sent in an emergency squad to shut down the Timeslip. Most of the creatures were killed pretty quickly; the members of the Nightside Gun Club couldn't believe their luck. They came running with every kind of gun you can think of, and the dinosaurs never stood a chance, poor bastards. The only reason the *T. rex* survived was because the big-game hunters spent too long squabbling over who had the right to go first. Walker claimed it for the Museum before they started a shooting war over it."

"How did they get it here?" said Bettie, standing very close to me. "I mean, look at it; that is big. Seriously big. There can't be that many tranquilliser darts in the world."

"Walker had one of his pet sorcerers put the thing in stasis while the Museum got its accommodations ready. Then the sorcerer transported it right into its cage. The Japanese have been pouring in to have their photographs taken with it ever since."

While we were watching the *T. rex*, and it was watching us, the uniformed Neanderthal had gone off and found the Museum's Director. He turned out to be one Percival Smythe-Herriot, a tall spindly figure in a shiny suit, with some of his breakfast still staining his waistcoat. He stamped to a halt before me and gave both Bettie and me a brief, professional, and utterly meaningless smile. He didn't offer to shake hands. He had a lean and hungry look, as though he was always ready to add a new exhibit to his beloved Museum and was already wondering how I would look stuffed, mounted, and put on display.

"John Taylor," he said, in a voice like someone trying to decide whether snail or octopus would make the least distressing starter. "Oh, yes; I know you. Or of you.

Trouble-maker. Or at the very least, someone trouble follows around like a devoted pet. Tell me what it is you want here, so I can help you find it, then escort you quickly to the nearest exit. Before something goes horribly and destructively wrong in my nice and carefully laid-out Museum."

"Are you going to let him talk to you like that?" said Bettie.

"Yes," I said. "I find his honesty and grasp of reality quite refreshing." I gave Percival my own professional smile and was quietly pleased to see him wince a little. "Walker sent me. I need to talk to the Collector."

"Oh, *him*. Yes . . . I'd never have let him in here, but Walker insisted. Part of the price tag for his help in acquiring the *T. rex*. Beware civil servants bearing gifts . . . I mean, giving the Collector free access to a museum is like letting a fox with a chain-saw into a hen-house. Thief! Grave-robber! *Amateur!* All the great historical treasures he's supposed to have, kept locked away so he can gloat over them in private, when by rights they should be on open display in my Museum! It doesn't bear thinking about. My doctor told me not to think about it; he said it was bad for my blood pressure. I have to take these little pink pills, and I'm always running out. I'd have the Collector thrown out . . . if I didn't think he'd kill me and all my staff and burn down the Museum as he left . . . So go ahead, talk to him. See if I care. I'm just the Director of this Museum. I can feel one of my heads coming on . . ."

"Where is the Collector?" I said patiently.

For the first time, Percival gave me a real smile. It wasn't at all a nice smile, but I had no doubt he meant it.

"Through there," he said, pointing at the *T. rex*'s cage. "There's a door, right in the middle of our artificial jungle. You'll find the Collector in his lair, on the other side of the door."

"Oh, joy," I said.

"Deep joy," said Bettie, staring in horrified fascination at the jungle in the cage. "The Collector really doesn't want visitors, does he? Why couldn't he have settled for a BEWARE OF THE DOG sign like anyone else?"

I looked at Percival. "I don't suppose . . ."

"My position is purely administrative," he said, still smiling his nasty smile. "You're on your own, Mr. Taylor."

He turned his back on us and strode away, snapping his fingers for the Neanderthal to follow him. I gave the cage my full attention. I wasn't sure if I really needed to see the Collector that badly. I moved slowly forward, going right up to the bars of the cage for a better look. Bettie stuck really close beside me. With my face next to the bars, I could feel the savage heat of the jungle. My bare skin smarted just from the feel of it.

The *T. rex* surged forward, exploding out of its cover, throwing broken vegetation in all directions. It crossed the intervening space in a few seconds, driven forward by its massive legs, and its slavering mouth slammed against the other side of the bars while I was still reacting to its first movement. The bars held, and the *T. rex* smashed its great head against them again and again, determined to reach me. I stumbled back, Bettie clinging desperately to my arm. The *T. rex* howled, a deafening roar of hate and frustration. The smell of rotting meat from its mouth was almost overpowering. I backed away some more, and Bettie turned and buried her face in my chest. I put my arms around her and held her. Both of us were shaking.

The *T. rex* snorted once, threateningly, and then turned its great bulk around and stalked back into the jungle. The ground really did tremble when it moved.

I was still holding Bettie. We were both breathing hard. I could feel her heart beating fast, close to mine. She raised her face to look at me. Her eyes were very big. I could feel her breath on my face. Her scent filled my head. Our faces were very close. It had been a long time since I'd held a woman this close to me.

It felt good.

I pushed her away gently, and immediately we were both two professional people again. I looked at the jungle. I thought I could make out the silhouette of the *T. rex*, lurking silently, concealed amongst the tall trees.

"Big, isn't it?" I said. "Fast, too."

"It smells of meat and murder," said Bettie. "It smells of death."

"It's a killer," I said.

"How the hell are we going to get past it?"

I looked at her. "You sure you want to try?"

"Hell yes! No oversized iguana is going to intimidate

122

me! Besides, never let anything distract you from following the story. First thing they teach you at the *Unnatural Inquirer*. Right after how to fill out an expenses claim and next-of-kin forms." She looked at me consideringly. "You couldn't just kill it, could you?"

"I think an awful lot of very well-connected people would be exceedingly upset."

"That's never stopped you before."

"True. But a *T. rex* is too damned special to kill unless I absolutely have to."

"So what do we do? Call in some of your more dangerous friends and allies for backup? Shotgun Suzie? Razor Eddie? The Grey Eidolon?"

"No," I said. "I solve my own problems."

I studied the artificial jungle, hot and sweaty and stinking under its artificial sun. Flies buzzed hungrily, along with foot-long dragonflies and other less familiar insects. The jungle on its own would be hard enough to take, even without the *T. rex*. I could see it more clearly now, shifting its weight slowly from one great leg to the other, its long tail twitching restlessly. It stood there, huge and menacing, waiting for me to try something. Waiting for its chance. There was no sign of the Collector's door; but it couldn't be far. The cage wasn't that big . . . I smiled slowly. The *T. rex* would know where the door was. It would know it was important. So it would put itself between me and the door. Which meant . . . My smile widened as I looked at the *T. rex*'s massive legs, and then at the space between them.

"That is a really unpleasant smile," said Bettie. "Whatever you're thinking, please stop it."

"I have a plan," I said.

"I'm really not going to like it, am I?"

"How fast can you run?" I said.

"Oh, no," she said. "You're not suggesting . . ."

"Oh, yes I am," I said.

I marched back to the cage bars, Bettie moving unhappily along with me. The *T. rex* stepped out into the open, grinning at me with its terrible jaws. The feeding arms high up on the barrel chest clutched spasmodically at the air. I reached into my coat-pocket and took out a flashbang. I gestured for Bettie to cover her eyes and ears, then tossed the flashbang into the cage. The *T. rex* started forward. I closed my eyes, covered my ears, and turned my head away, and the flashbang exploded, filling the world with a fierce incandescent glare. I could still see it through my clenched-shut eyes. The *T. rex* screamed like a steam whistle. I turned back, grabbed Bettie's hand, and we squeezed quickly between the steel bars. Designed to keep the *T. rex* in, not people out. The *T. rex* stamped its great feet up and down, swinging its wedge-shaped head back and forth, trying to shake off the pain in its dazzled eyes. And I ran straight at the creature, with Bettie pounding gamely along at my side.

The heat hit me like a blast furnace, and the stench was almost unbearable. The *T. rex* knew we were coming, but it was too confused to place us. It snapped at the empty air, the heavy jaws slamming together like a man-trap. I headed for the gap between its legs. I think it sensed how close we were, because the great head came sweeping down. Bettie and I ran straight between its wide-set legs and out the other side, hardly having to duck at all. The *T. rex*'s head smashed into the ground as it missed us.

By the time the *T. rex* had shaken off its daze and its new headache, and got itself turned around, I'd already found the Collector's door and got it open. It wasn't even locked, the smug bastard. I pushed Bettie through and followed her in. I turned to shut the door, and there was the *T. rex*, shrieking with rage as it lurched towards the door. I blew a raspberry at it, and shut the door in its face.

Inside the Collector's lair, it was blessedly cool. I took a moment to get my breath back. I wasn't worried about the door. Any door the Collector trusted to guard his treasures could take care of itself. I looked around, while Bettie got her breathing back under control and cursed me with a whole series of baby swear-words. The Collector's new domain looked a lot like his old one. It stretched away in all directions, for as far as the eye could follow, and most of it was pretty damned hard on the eye. Walls, floor, and ceiling were all painted in bright primary Technicolor, with gaudy hanging silks to separate one area from another. The Collector's tastes had been formed in the psychedelic sixties, and he never really got over it.

But whereas his old collection up on the Moon had all

been stored away in rows and rows of wooden crates, here they were all set out in the open, presented carefully on rows and rows of glass shelving. Jewels and weapons, books and documents, machines and artifacts from all of recorded history. I recognised a few of the bigger items, like the wooden horse of Troy, and a half-burned giant Wicker Man with a dead policeman inside it, under carefully arranged spotlights; but I didn't have to know what the rest were to know they were important. They all but radiated glamour.

I looked round sharply as the Collector's security staff arrived, pattering across the bright blue floor towards us. Gleaming humanoid robots from some future Chinese civilisation, graceful and deadly with steel-clawed hands, and stylised cat faces complete with jutting metal whiskers. Their slit-pupilled eyes glowed green. A dozen of the robots moved swiftly to surround us, and I gestured quickly for Bettie to stand still. The robots hadn't been sent to kill us, or I'd never have heard them coming. Bettie stood firm, glaring about her.

"Call them off, Collector," I said, in a loud and carrying voice. "Or I'll turn them into scrap metal."

"You never did have any respect for other people's property, Taylor."

The cat robots fell back silently, to allow the Collector to approach. A pudgy, middle-aged man with a flushed face and beady little eyes, wearing a wraparound Roman toga, white with purple trimmings. There were knife holes and old blood stains on the toga's front. Lots of them.

"Do you like it?" he said, stopping a respectful distance away. "A new acquisition. The robe the Emperor Caligula was wearing when he was assassinated by his own security people. Partly because he was a monster, but mostly because he embarrassed the hell out of them." He looked at me, then at Bettie, who I now noticed was wearing a deep burgundy evening gown, with her long dark hair tumbling in ringlets to her shoulders. Her curved horns gleamed dully under the bright lights. The Collector smiled suddenly. "They've been feeding that *T. rex* too much; he's getting slow and sloppy. I shall have to have words with that little snot Percival. What do you want here, Taylor?"

I looked around, evading the subject for the moment. Some things you need to sneak up on, and ease into. Especially when you've known the Collector as long as I have.

"I like what you've done with the place," I said. "Up on the Moon, you had everything packed away in boxes. You thinking of opening up to the public?"

"They wish," said the Collector. "What's mine is mine, and not for other eyes. But I had something of an epiphany during the Lilith War; it reminded me of how short life can be, and the necessity for enjoying things while you still can. It's not enough just to own things, any more; I need to be able to walk amongst them, enjoy them, savour them. And I do. What do you want, Taylor?"

"I need a favour," I said. "And you do owe me, Mark."

He looked at me for a long moment, but in the end he looked away first. He seemed suddenly older, and tired.

"How much am I expected to pay for my sins against you?"

I could sense Bettie's ears pricking up, as she realised we were talking about secret, important things, but I didn't feel like enlightening her.

"Only you can answer that," I said. "Just tell me what I need to know, and I'll leave."

"I should kill you," he said, almost casually.

"You could try," I said, easily.

"This is about the Afterlife Recording, isn't it? I haven't got it. Heard about it, of course. The whole damned Nightside is buzzing with news of it, mostly inaccurate, and all the little collectors and speculators are driving themselves crazy running in circles, chasing down every rumour . . ."

"But not you?" I said.

"I want it. And when I'm good and ready, I'll go and get it. But right now I'm busy with something . . . something important. I have yet to be convinced that the Recording is the genuine article. But whether it's the real deal or not, I will have it, because it's a unique item, and it belongs here with me, as someone who will appreciate it . . . What is that woman doing?"

I looked around. Bettie had a small camera in her hands. I reached out and took it away from her.

"Give that back!" she said hotly. "It belongs to the paper! I had to sign for it!"

"Restrain yourself," I said. "We're guests here."

"Oh, but look at all the lovely things he's got," said Bettie, pouting in a very winning way. "The world deserves to know what's here!"

"No they don't," said the Collector. He gave me a thoughtful look. "Is she your latest?"

"No," I said. "I'm still with Suzie."

"Oh. Nice horns." He gave me a hard look. "You always were more trouble than you were worth, Taylor. You know how long it took me to regrow my leg after those insects gnawed it off? All because of you? Give me one good reason why I shouldn't have my lovely cat robots kill you, stuff you, and put you on display?"

"Because I'm my father's son."

"You always did fight dirty, John." He smiled briefly. "The sins of the father . . ."

"And the mother," I said. "And the man who put them together."

"Walker had sons," said the Collector. "Charles had you. And I . . . have my collection. Funny how things turn out. Get out of here, Taylor. I don't have the Afterlife Recording, and I don't know who has. Leave. And don't come looking for me again. I won't be here."

He turned and walked away, followed by his cat robots. Bettie looked at me.

"What was that all about?"

"The past," I said. "And how it always ends up haunting the present. Let's go."

"You're sure he doesn't have it, hidden away somewhere?"

"He wouldn't lie to me," I said.

We headed back to the door. Bettie was still frowning thoughtfully.

"Once we're back in the artificial jungle, we've still got to face one very pissed-off *Tyrannosaurus rex*. How are we going to get past it this time?"

"Don't worry," I said. "I'll think of something."

And I did.

# FIVE

*The Devil's in the Details*

Back out on the Nightside streets again, we still carried the smell of the jungle with us. A harsh and murky mixture of sweat, rotting vegetation, and *T. rex* musk. It could have been my imagination, but people on the street seemed to be giving me even more room than usual. I felt like buying half a dozen air fresheners and hanging them round my neck. I did my best to rise above the situation, while debating what to do next with the delightful Bettie Divine.

"I still don't get it," she said, a bit pettishly. She was holding my arm again. "Why isn't the Collector out chasing round the Nightside, trying to grab the Afterlife Recording for himself? He said he wanted it."

"He also said he was busy with something," I said. "Odd, that; he didn't say what with. He's never been bashful with me before; usually can't wait to boast about what he's up to . . . Still, he's the Collector. Which means he's always busy with something."

"Unless . . . he's scared of someone else who's after the Recording," said Bettie. "You, perhaps?"

"I'd like to think so, but no. It would have to be someone really bad, and really powerful. The Collector is a Major Player in his own right, and he doesn't scare easily."

"Walker?"

"You have a point there," I admitted. I was getting used to walking arm in arm with Bettie. It felt good, natural. "Could Walker have been lying to us, to hide the fact he already had the DVD? No, I don't think so. He would have told me if he'd had it, if only to put me in my place. And his reasons for wanting me to find it before anyone else sounded pretty good to me."

"You mean the angels?" said Bettie.

"Please," I said. "Let us not use the a-word in public."

"All right, if it isn't Walker, then who? Razor Eddie?"

I shook my head. "He might be the Punk God of the Straight Razor, but Eddie's never been very interested in religion. In fact, he's pretty much the only god all the other Beings on the Street of the Gods are afraid of."

"How about the Lord of Thorns, then?"

"You have been doing your homework, haven't you? No, he's still recovering from the Lilith War and the trauma of finding out he's not who he thought he was."

"You know everyone, don't you?" Bettie said admiringly. "Who did he think he was?"

"Overseer of the Nightside."

Bettie thought about that. "If the Lord of Thorns isn't watching over us, who is?"

"Good question," I said. "Lot of people are still arguing about that."

She gave me a sly, sideways look. "Lot of people say you could have been King of the Nightside, if you'd wanted."

I smiled. "You shouldn't listen to gossip."

"Don't be silly, darling! That's my job!"

"Damn," I said, as a thought occurred to me.

"You're frowning, John, and I do wish you wouldn't. It usually means you've suddenly thought of something unpleasant, spooky, and probably downright dangerous."

"Right on all three counts," I said. "There is one man the Collector is afraid of, and quite rightly, too. Anyone with any sense is afraid of the Removal Man."

Bettie pulled her arm out of mine and stopped dead in the street. I stopped with her. She gave me a hard look.

"Hold everything, reverse gear, go previous. Are you having fun with me, John? Thinking I'll believe anything simply because it's you saying it? The Removal Man is just an urban legend. Isn't he?"

"Unfortunately, no," I said.

"But . . . I don't know anyone who's seen him, or even claimed to have seen him! The *Unnatural Inquirer*'s been offering really quite serious money for a *photo* . . . No-one's ever come forward."

"Because they're too scared," I said. "You don't mess with the Removal Man; not if you like existing."

"Have you ever met him?" said Bettie, her voice carefully casual.

"No," I said. "And I was hoping to keep it that way. I don't think he approves of me. And people and things the Removal Man disapproves of have this unfortunate tendency to disappear without a trace. The Removal Man has made it his personal crusade to wander the Nightside anonymously, removing all the things and people that offend him. Removing, as in making them vanish so completely that even really Major Players have been unable to confirm exactly what it is he's done with them."

"He removes people from reality because they offend him?" said Bettie.

"Pretty much." I started off down the street again, and Bettie came along with me. Not holding my arm. "Basically, the Removal Man drops the hammer on people if he considers them to be a threat to the Nightside, or the world in general . . . or because who or what they are offends his particular moral beliefs. Judge, jury, and executioner, though no-one's ever seen him do it."

"Like . . . Jessica Sorrow?" said Bettie, frowning.

"No . . . Jessica made bits of the world disappear because she didn't believe in them, and her disbelief was stronger than their reality. Very scary lady. Luckily she sleeps a lot of the time. No, the Removal Man chooses what he wants to disappear. No-one's ever been able to bring any of his victims back; and a whole lot of pretty powerful people have tried . . . I've never heard a single guess at his name, or who he used to be before he came here and took on his role. And this in a place that runs on rumours. He's a mystery, and all the signs are he likes it that way."

"You are seriously spooking me out, sweetie," said Bettie. "Are you sure he's involved with this?"

"No; but it sounds right. The Afterlife Recording is exactly the sort of thing that would attract the Removal Man's attention. Rumour has it he only ever reveals his identity to those he's about to remove, and not always then. There's some evidence he can work close up, or from a distance. Certainly he doesn't give a damn about celebrity, or notoriety, or even reward. He works for his own satisfaction. It's hard to be a shadowy urban legend in a place full of marvels and nightmares, but he's managed it. I'm almost jealous."

"I did hear one rumour," Bettie said carefully. "That he once tried to remove Walker . . . but it didn't take."

I shrugged. "If it did happen, Walker's never mentioned it. I suppose it's possible that Walker secretly approves of the Removal Man. In fact, it wouldn't surprise me if the Removal Man did the occasional job for him, on the quiet, disappearing people that Walker considered a threat to the status quo . . . No . . . No, that can't be right."

"Why not?"

"Because Walker would have sent the Removal Man after me long ago."

Bettie laughed and took my arm again. "You don't half fancy yourself, John Taylor. Any idea where the Removal Man might have gained his power?"

"The same way everybody else does," I said. "He made a deal with Someone or Something. Makes you wonder what he might have paid in exchange . . . I suppose it could be the Removal Man, or his patron, who's been interfering with my gift. I really do hope it isn't the Devil again."

"I could ask Mummy for you," said Bettie. "She still has contacts with the Old Firm."

"Think I'll pass," I said.

Bettie shrugged easily. "Suit yourself. You know, if we don't get to Pen Donavon before the Removal Man does, we could lose both him and his DVD. And my paper has paid a lot of money for that DVD."

"It might not be the Removal Man," I said. "I was thinking aloud. Speculating. I could be wrong. I have been before. In fact, this is one time I'd really like to be wrong."

"He worries you, doesn't he?"

"Damn right he does."

"Tell you what," said Bettie, snuggling up against me and squeezing my arm companionably against her breast. "When you want the very latest gossip on anything, ask a reporter. Or better yet, a whole bunch of reporters! Come with me, sweetie; I'm taking you to the Printer's Devil."

•　　•　　•

Luckily, the Printer's Devil turned out to be a bar where reporters congregated when they were off work; *printer's devil* being old-time slang for a typesetter. The bar catered almost exclusively to journalists, a private place where they could let their hair down amongst their own kind and share the kinds of stories that would never see print. Situated half-way down a gloomy side street, the Printer's Devil was an old place, and almost defiantly old-fashioned. It had a black-and-white timbered Tudor front, complete with jutting gables and a hanging sign showing a medieval Devil, complete with scarlet skin, goatee beard, and a pair of horns on his forehead that reminded my very much of Bettie's, operating a simple printing press. Reporters can be very literal, when they're off duty.

Bettie breezed through the door like a visiting princess, and I wandered in after her. The interior turned out to be equally old-fashioned, with sawdust on the floor, horse brasses over the bar, and a low ceiling with exposed beams. A dozen different beers on tap, with distressingly twee olde-worlde names, like *Langford's Exceedingly Old Speckled Hen. Taste that albumen!* A chalked sign offered traditional pub grub—chips with everything. And not a modern appliance anywhere in sight, including, thankfully, a juke-box. There was a deafening roar of chatter from the mob of shabby and shifty characters crowded round the tables and filling the booths, and the atmosphere was hot, sweaty, and smoky. There was so much nicotine in the air you could practically chew it. A great clamour of greeting went up as Bettie was recognised, only to die quickly away to a strained silence as they recognised me. Bettie smiled sweetly around her.

"It's all right," she said. "He's with me."

The reporters immediately turned their backs on us and resumed their conversations as though nothing had happened. One of their own had vouched for me, and that was all it took. Bettie headed for the crowded bar, and I moved quickly after her. She smiled and waved and shouted the odd cheery greeting at those around her, and everyone smiled and waved and shouted back. Clearly, Bettie was a very popular girl. At the bar, I asked her what she was drinking, and she batted her heavy eyelashes and asked for a Horny Red Devil. Which turned out to be gin, vodka, and Worcester sauce, with a wormwood-and-brimstone chaser. To each their own. At least it didn't come with a little umbrella in it. I ordered a Coke. A real Coke, and none of that diet nonsense. Bettie looked at me.

"Never when I'm working," I said solemnly.

"Really? It's the other way round with me, darling. I couldn't face this job sober." She smiled happily. "I notice the bartender didn't ask you to pay for these drinks. Don't you ever pay for anything?"

"I pay my way at Strangefellows," I said. "The owner is a friend."

"Ooh; Strangefellows, sweetie! Yes, I've heard about that place! There are all kinds of stories about what goes on in Strangefellows!"

"And most of them are true. It is the oldest pub in the world, after all."

"Will you take me there after we've finished with this assignment? I'd love to go dancing at Strangefellows. We could relax and get squiffy together. I might even show you my tail."

"We'll probably end up there, at some point," I said. "Most of my cases take me there, eventually."

The bartender slammed our drinks down on the highly polished wooden bar top, then backed away quickly. I didn't care for the man, and I think he could tell. He was one of those stout jolly types, with a red face and a ready smile, always there to make cheerful conversation when all you want is to drink in peace. Probably referred to himself as Mine Host. I gave him a meaningful look, and he retreated to the other end of the bar to polish some glasses that didn't need polishing.

"Can't take you anywhere," said Bettie.

Behind the bar hung a giveaway calendar supplied by the *Unnatural Inquirer*, with a large photo featuring the charms of a very well-developed young lady whose clothes had apparently fallen off. At the bottom of the page was the paper's current slogan: ARE YOU GETTING IT REGU-LARLY? Some rather shrunken-looking meat pies were on display in a glass case, but one look was all it took to convince me I would rather tear my tongue out. A stuffed-and-mounted fox head winked at me, and I snarled back. Animals should know their place. Not a lot further down the bar, an old-fashioned manual typewriter was being operated by the invisible hands of a real ghost writer. I'd met it once before, at the *Night Times* offices, and was tempted to make a remark about spirits not being served here, but rose above it. I leaned over towards the type-writer, and the clacking keys paused.

"Any recent news on the whereabouts of the Afterlife Recording?"

Words quickly formed on the page, reading *Future's cloudy. Ask again later.*

I persuaded Bettie to hurry her drink, politely evaded her attempts to chat, bond, or get personal, and finally we moved away from the bar to mingle with the assembled reporters. With Bettie as my native guide, we passed eas-ily from group to group, with me doing my best to be courteous and charming. I needn't have bothered. The re-porters only had eyes for Bettie, who was in full flirt mode—all squeaky voice, fluttering lashes, and a bit of laying on of hands where necessary. Bettie was currently wearing a smart white blouse with half the buttons un-done, over a simple black skirt, fish-net stockings, and high heels. Her horns showed clearly on her forehead, per-haps because she felt safe and at home here.

All the journalists seemed quite willing to talk about the Afterlife Recording; they'd all heard something, or swore they had. No-one wanted to appear out of the loop or left behind in company like this. Unfortunately, most of what they had to tell us turned out to be vague, mis-leading, or contradictory. Pen Donavon had been seen here, there, and everywhere, and already all sorts of people were offering copies of the DVD for sale. Only to be expected in the Nightside, where people have been known to rip off a new idea while it was still forming in the originator's mind. Rumours were already circulating that some people had managed to view what was on the DVD and had immediately Raptured right out of their clothes. Though whether Up or Down remained unconfirmed.

Bettie stopped at a table, and greeted one particular reporter with particular cold venom, along with a stare that would have poisoned a rattlesnake at forty paces. He seemed bright and cheerful enough, in an irredeemably seedy sort of way. He wore a good suit badly, and had a diamond tie-pin big enough to be classed as an offensive weapon.

"Aren't you going to introduce us?" I said innocently to Bettie.

She sniffed loudly. "John, darling, this particular gusset stain is Rick Aday, reporter for the *Night Times*."

"Investigative reporter," he corrected her easily, flashing perfect but somewhat yellow teeth in a big smile. He put out a hand for me to shake. I looked at it, and he took it back again. "You must have seen my by-line, Mr. Taylor, I've written lots of stories about you: *Rick Aday; Trouble Is My Middle Name*."

"No it isn't," Bettie said briskly. "It's Cedric."

Aday shot her a venomous glare. "Better than yours, *Delilah*."

"Lick my scabs!"

"They used to date," another of the reporters confided quietly to me. I nodded. I'd already guessed that.

"I've been hot on the trail of the Afterlife Recording for some time now," Aday said loftily. "Pursuing several quite credible leads, actually. Just waiting for a phone call from one of my extremely clued-in informants, then I'll be off to make Mr. Donavon a generous offer for his DVD."

"You can't!" Bettie snapped immediately. "My paper has a legitimate contract with Pen Donavon, granting us exclusive rights to his material!"

Aday just grinned at her. "Finders keepers, losers read about it in the *Night Times*."

"I suppose all's fair in love and publishing," I said, and Bettie actually hissed at me.

I moved away, to allow Bettie and her old flame to exchange harsh words in private. I'd noticed that the nearby wall boasted a whole series of framed cartoons and caricatures of noted Nightside personalities. Good likenesses, if often harsh, exaggerated, and downright cruel. They were all signed with a name I recognised. Bozie's work was well-known in the Nightside, appearing in all the best papers and magazines. He excelled at bringing out a subject's worst attributes and qualities, making them seem monstrous and laughable at the same time. Those depicted usually gritted their teeth and smiled as best they could, because you weren't anybody in the Nightside unless you'd been caricatured by Bozie.

There were rumours that Bozie had been known to accept quite large sums of money to kill a particular creation of his before the public got to see it. No-one mentioned blackmail, of course. Thus are reputations made in the Nightside.

I've never approved of needless cruelty. You should save it for when it's really necessary.

I moved slowly along the wall, checking out the various pen-and-ink creations in their softwood frames. All the usual suspects were there. Walker, of course, looking very sinister with more than a hint of in-breeding. Julien Advent, impossibly noble, complete with halo and stigmata. The Sonic Assassin, in his sixties greatcoat, gnawing on a human thigh-bone while making a rude gesture at the viewer. And . . . Shotgun Suzie. My Suzie. I stopped before the caricature and studied it impassively. Bozie had made her look like a monster. All fetishy black leathers and unfeasibly big breasts, with a face like an axe murderer. He'd exaggerated every detail of her looks to make her seem ugly and crazy. This wasn't just a caricature; it was an assault on her character. It was an insult.

"Like it?" said a lazy voice at my side. I looked round, and there was the artist himself—the famous or more properly infamous Bozie. A tall, gangling sort, in scruffy blue jeans and a T-shirt bearing an idealised image of his own face. He had long, floppy hair, dark, intense eyes, and an openly mocking smile. He gestured languidly at Suzie's caricature. "It is for sale, you know. If you want it?"

I had a feeling I knew how this was going to play out,

but I went along with it. "All right," I said. "How much?"

"Oh, for you . . . Let's say a round hundred thousand pounds." He giggled suddenly. "A bargain at the price. Or you can leave it here, for all the world to see. Who knows how many papers and magazines might want to run it?"

"I've got a better idea," I said.

"Oh, do tell."

I hit the glass covering the caricature with my fist, and it shattered immediately, jagged pieces falling out of the frame. Bozie stepped quickly backwards, his hands held protectively out before him. I tore the caricature out of the frame, and ripped it up, letting the pieces fall to the floor at my feet. Bozie goggled at me, torn between shock and outrage.

"You . . . You can't do that!" he managed finally.

"I just did."

"I'll sue!"

I smiled. "Good luck with that."

"I can always draw another one," Bozie said spitefully. "An even better one!"

"If you do," I said, "I will find you."

Bozie couldn't meet my gaze. He looked around him, hoping for help or support, but no-one wanted to know. He sat down at his table again, still not looking at me, and sulked. I went back to Bettie's table, and sat beside her. She patted me on the arm.

"That was very sweet, dear. Though a bit harsh on poor Bozie."

"Hell," I said. "I saved his life. Suzie would have shot him on sight. She doesn't have my innate courtesy and restraint."

There was a certain amount of coughing around the table, and then everyone went back to their discussion on what the Afterlife Recording might actually contain. The suggestions were many and varied, but eventually boiled down to the following:

1. There was a new rebel angel in Heaven, rebelling against the long silence of millennia to finally broadcast the truth about Humanity. Why we were created, what our true purpose is, and why we are born to suffer.

2. It was a transmission from Hell, saying that God is dead and they can prove it. Satan runs our world, tormenting us for his pleasure. Which would explain a lot.

3. An exact date for the final war between Heaven and Hell. Broadcast now because . . . it's all about to kick off.

4. There is a Heaven, but it's only for the innocent animals. People just die.

5. There is a Heaven, but no Hell.

6. There is a Hell, but no Heaven.

7. It's all bullshit.

There was a lot of nodding and raising of glasses at that last one. Once the subject of the DVD's contents had been thoroughly exhausted, I took it upon myself to raise the possibility of the Removal Man's involvement. Everyone perked up immediately and tumbled over each other to provide anecdotes and stories they'd come across but had been unable to get printed. Because no-one could prove anything.

"Remember Jonnie Reggae?" said Rick Aday. "Used to headline at the old Shell Beach Club? Rumour has it he vanished right in the middle of his set because the Removal Man was in the audience and decided his material was offensive. Management was livid. They'd booked Jonnie for the whole season."

"He's supposed to have made a house disappear, on Blaiston Street," said Lovett, from the *Nightside Observer*.

"Actually, no," I said. "That was me."

There was some more awkward coughing before Bettie determinedly got the conversation back on course.

"Remember Bully Boy Bates?" she said brightly. "Used to run a protection racket in the sweat-shop districts? Julien Advent was just getting ready to run an exposé on him in the *Times*, then suddenly didn't need to because Bates and all his cronies had gone missing. Or how about that alien predator, that disguised itself as an ambulance so it could eat the people put into it? That was the Removal Man. Supposedly. He has done some good."

"Yes," said Aday, drawing the word out till it sounded more like no, "but on the other hand, look what he did to the first incarnation of the Caligula Club. You know, that place that caters to all the more extreme forms of sexuality. Lots of people having a good time, according to their lights, all of it adult and consensual . . . but too much for the Removal Man's puritan tastes. He made the whole Club disappear, along with everyone in it. Just like that! Which is why the current version of the Club has such heavy-duty protections, and it's so hard to get in. Or so they tell me . . ."

And then the whole place fell suddenly silent as the door crashed open and General Condor entered, along with a dozen heavily armed and armoured body-guards. They made sure the place was secure and only then put their guns away. The General strode forward and looked the place over. He didn't appear especially impressed—by the bar or its customers. He was still wearing his Space Fleet uniform, complete with golden bars on his shoulders and rows of medal ribbons on his chest. He had the look of the old soldier, the calm steady look that said he'd seen a lot of men die, and your death wouldn't bother him in the least.

"John Taylor," he said, his heavy deliberate voice crashing into the hush. "I want him."

I stood up. "Get in line," I said. "I'm busy."

He looked me over, then surprised me by smiling

briefly. If anything, it made him look even more dangerous. "I need to talk to you, Taylor. And you need to listen."

I looked at him, then at the body-guards, and then at
the reporters, all staring at us with wide eyes, impressed
out of their minds. That settled it. I couldn't let them
down. I nodded to the General, who gestured stiffly at a
corner booth. The young man and woman sitting in it
got the message, and vacated immediately, leaving their
drinks behind. The General sat down stiffly in the booth,
and I went over to join him. Bettie wanted to come with
me, but I was firm. She pouted and stamped her little
foot, but she did stay put. I sat down facing the General,
and his body-guards moved quickly to form a defensive
barrier between the booth and the rest of the bar, their
hands resting on the butts of their guns. The reporters
turned up their noses at them and ostentatiously went
back to their own conversations.

I looked thoughtfully at the General. "I'm not sure I
want to hear anything you have to say, General. I'm not
the military type, I have problems with authority figures,
and I don't play well with others."

"A lot of people don't want to hear what's good for
them. The order of things in the Nightside is changing.
The Authorities are gone, and someone has to replace
them before this whole place tears itself apart fighting
over the spoils. I can put the Nightside on the right
course, John. Make it a place to be proud of. I have support from many fine and influential people, but I could
use you on my side."

"Why me?" I said, genuinely curious.

"Don't be disingenuous." General Condor sighed tiredly and leaned forward across the table. "You've been a force for good in the Nightside. You help people. You've even been known to dispense your own kind of justice when necessary. Help me to save the Nightside from its own excesses."

"You can't force change in the Nightside," I said. Something in me warmed to the General's blunt honesty, if not his cause, so I gave him the truth, and not what he wanted to hear. "The Nightside is what it wants to be. It's fought wars with Heaven and Hell for the right to go its own way. The best you can do, the best any of us can do, is encourage change for the better, one small step at a time."

"The Nightside has had thousands of years to grow up," said the General. "If it was capable of saving itself, it would have done so by now. It needs a firm hand on the tiller, it needs control and discipline imposed from above, like any military unit that's gone bad. Walker tried, but he was only ever the Authorities' puppet. He can't run things on his own. He must be replaced."

"Good luck with that," I said.

He smiled again. "If I thought it would be easy, I wouldn't be here talking to you."

"He has the Voice," I said.

"It doesn't work on you," said the General.

I raised an eyebrow. "You want me to kiss him on the cheek while I'm there?"

"I want you to do what's right. What's best for everyone."

"Even I don't know what that is," I said. "And I've been looking for it a lot longer than you have."

"If you're not with me, you're against me," General Condor said flatly. "And if you don't choose a side soon, one may be chosen for you."

I smiled. "Good luck with that, too."

He laughed briefly, quietly. "I could have used a man like you on my flagship, John. You won't bend or yield for anyone, will you?"

"Why is this so important to you?" I said, seriously. "You haven't been here long. Why this need to save the Nightside from itself?"

"I have to do something," said the General. "I couldn't save my Fleet. I couldn't save my men. I have to do *something* . . ."

He got up from the table, and I stood up with him. He offered me his hand, and I shook it. The General left the Printer's Devil with his body-guards, and I went back to join Bettie Divine.

"Well?" she said, almost bouncing up and down in her seat. "What was that all about?"

"Just politics," I said. "Nightside style. Anything new or useful come up, while I was gone?"

"But John . . . !"

"Move along," I said.

"You need to talk to the Collector," said Rick Aday.

"Been there, done that," said Bettie.

"Oh." Aday looked crest-fallen for a moment, and then brightened again. "All right, how about the Cardinal? You know, used to run the Vatican's Extremely Forbidden Library. Until they discovered he was sneaking things out for his own private collection. Had to go on the run and ended up here, where he's supposed to have built up a really impressive hoard of religious artifacts. He's your man. If anyone's got close to the Afterlife Recording, it'll be the Cardinal."

"Good call," I said. "Bettie, I think we need to pay the Cardinal a visit. It's been a while since I scared the shit out of him, for the good of his soul."

"Ah," said Aday, smiling craftily. "Word is, he's moved, and taken his collection with him. Hardly anyone knows where he is now."

"But you know," said Bettie.

"Of course."

"Oh, please, please, Ricky sweetie, tell us where he is," said Bettie, giving him the full fluttering eye-lashes treatment. "I'll be ever so grateful, I promise."

Aday smirked triumphantly. "And what makes you think I'll just give up a valuable piece of information like that?"

"Because she asked you nicely," I said. "I won't."

Aday gave us the Cardinal's new address, and directions on how to find it. Bettie and I left the Printer's Devil. She waved good-bye and blew kisses in all directions. I didn't. I had my dignity to consider.

# SIX

*Heated Emotions from Unexpected Directions*

It's hard to maintain a reputation for being grim and mysterious when you're accompanied by a brightly clad young thing, skipping merrily along at your side, holding your hand, and smiling sweetly on one and all. Still, it felt good to have Bettie with me. Her constant enthusiasm and optimism helped relieve a weight and burden I hadn't even realised I was carrying. She made me feel . . . alive again.

Following Rick Aday's directions, we were heading into one of the more seedy areas of the Nightside, where the narrow streets are lined with scruffy little shops and emporiums, where half the street-lights never work, and most of the neon signs have letters missing. The kind of shop where there's a sale on all the year round, where they specialise in only fairly convincing knock-offs of whatever brand-names are currently fashionable or in demand, where the buyer had better not only beware, but carry a large stick and count his fingers on the way out. Shops that sell tarnished dreams and tacky nightmares, misleading miracles and wondrous devices, most of whose batteries have run down. Bottom feeders, in other words; tourist traps, and home to every cheap and nasty con you can think of. The crowds were just as heavy here, jostling each other off the pavement and shouldering each other out of the way. Everyone loves a bargain.

And then, suddenly, everyone was yelling and running. I stopped and looked quickly around me. I hadn't done anything. The crowds scattered quickly, to reveal Queen Helena striding down the street, staring grimly at me, at the head of her own small army of sycophants, followers, and armed men. I stood my ground, doing my best to appear casual and unconcerned. Bettie stuck close to me, quivering with excitement. Queen Helena finally crashed to a halt right in front of me, fixing me with her cold faraway eyes. She was wrapped from head to toe in thick white furs, parting now as she struck a regal pose, to reveal glimpses of blue-white skin. She looked like someone who had died and then been buried in the permafrost. There was no warmth anywhere in her harsh, regal features, but her eyes blazed with arrogant superiority. She looked at me expectantly, waiting for me to kneel or bow or offer to kiss her hand. So I ignored her completely, concentrating on the colourful figures who'd moved forward out of her army to back her up.

"Take a good look," I said cheerfully to Bettie. "It's not every day you see so many prominent members of the Exiles Club out in public. Mostly, these aristocratic nobodies prefer to skulk inside their very own members-only club, addressing each other by their old titles because they're the only ones that will. They trade grievances about lost lands and abandoned kingdoms, how nobody recognises true quality in this dreadful place, and how you just can't get good servants any more.

"The bald, stooped, and vulturelike figure to Queen Helena's left is Zog, King of the Pixies. Word has it he's been wearing those scabby feathered robes ever since he turned up here thirty years ago, and he hasn't washed them once. Try to avoid standing downwind. Queen Mab herself kicked him out of the Fae Court, for using glamour spells to lie with human women. He always killed them after he'd had his way with them, but Mab didn't care about that. Sex outside their race is one of the Fae's greatest taboos. So here he is now, stripped of his glamour, just another rapist and murderer with a title that means nothing at all.

"Next to him we have His Altitude Tobermoret, monarch of all he surveyed in Far Afrique. A dark and distinguished gentleman indeed, in his zebra-hide suit and his lion-claw necklace. Tobermoret used to be War Chief of an entire continent, until his people realised he was starting wars and rebellions just for the fun of it. He did so love sending young men out to die while he sat at his ease in a tent overlooking the battle-field, enjoying the show. I did hear tell his people castrated him before they shoved him through the Timeslip, which is why he's always in such a bad temper.

"On Queen Helena's other side is Prince Xerxes the Murder Monarch. And yes, those really are preserved human eyes and organs and other bits and pieces hanging from all those chains he's got wrapped around him. Though given how much he's gone to seed since he got here, one can't help wishing he'd wear something else apart from just the chains. He practises necromancy, the magic of murder. Partly because it's traditional where he comes from, but mostly because he gets off on it. Though he's learned to leave the tourists alone ever since Walker had a quiet word with him.

"And finally, next to Xerxes we have King Artur, of Sinister Albion. For every glorious dream, there's a nightmare equivalent, somewhere in the time-streams. For every helping hand, a kick in the face. In Sinister Albion, Merlin Satanspawn decided to embrace his father's qualities instead of rejecting them, and brought up young Artur in his own awful image. Under their direction, Camelot became a place of blood and horror, where knights in terrible armour feasted on the hearts of good men, and Albion blazed from end to end with burning Wicker Men. The only reason I haven't killed Artur on general principles, is because I've been too busy with other things."

I smiled at Queen Helena. "I think that's it. Have I missed anything important?"

"You do so love the sound of your own voice, Taylor," said Queen Helena. "And you will address me as Your Majesty."

"That'll be the day," I said cheerfully. "What do you want with me, Helena? Or are you just taking the Exiles out for a walk?"

It took her a moment to work out how to answer me. She wasn't used to open defiance, let alone ridicule. "You were seen," she said finally, "talking with the General Condor. You will tell me what you talked about. What you decided. What plans were made. Tell me everything, and I shall make a place for you in my army. Power and riches shall be yours. I could use a man like you, Taylor."

"Ah, what it is to be popular and desired," I said. "The leadership of the Nightside is up for grabs, and suddenly everyone wants me on their side. Flattering, but . . . annoying. I'm busy right now, Helena. And I have to say, even if I wasn't . . . there isn't enough gold in the Nightside to persuade me to work for you, let alone this bunch of titled scumbags."

"Why do you say these things to me?" said Queen Helena. "When you know I will kill you for it?"

I shrugged. "I think you bring out the worst in me. There's some shit I simply will not put up with."

Her arms came out from under her robes, bulging tech implants already thrusting up through the blue-white skin. Dull grey gun muzzles orientated on me. Zog raised a withered arm to show off a beaten-copper glove with sharpened claws, buzzing with arcane energies. Tobermoret slammed the end of his long wooden staff on the pavement, and all the runes and sigils carved deep into the wood began to glow with a disquieting light. Xerxes produced a pair of long, curved daggers with serrated edges that looked more like butcher's tools. He grinned at me, showing off dull brown teeth filed to points. And Artur's bleak and brutal battle armour slowly came to life, its metal parts creeping and crawling over him, muttering to themselves in hissing otherworldly voices. Behind his blank steel helmet, his eyes glowed like corpsefires.

And behind Queen Helena and her Exiles, armed and armoured men hefted their various weapons, impatient for the order to attack.

Bettie Divine made quiet whimpering noises and looked like she'd rather be anywhere else than here, but still she held her ground at my side.

I took a sudden deliberate step forward, so I could look Queen Helena right in the eye. "I could have been King of the Nightside if I'd wanted. I didn't. Did you really think I'd bend the knee and bow my head to such as you?"

"I have powerful allies!" said Queen Helena. "I have an army in waiting! I have potent weapons!"

I laughed in her face. "You really think that's going to make a difference? *I'm John Taylor.*"

Queen Helena held my gaze longer than I'd thought she would, but in the end she looked away and stepped back a pace, her tech implants ducking back under her skin. I looked unhurriedly about me, and the Exiles fell back, too, powering down their weapons. Their followers stirred uneasily, looking at each other. Some of them were muttering my name.

Because I was John Taylor; and there was no telling what I might do. It was all I could do to keep from smiling.

And then, just when it was all going so well, Uptown Taffy Lewis came storming up the street from the other direction, at the head of his own small army of bully-boys, body-guards, and enforcers. All of them heavily armed. I turned my back on Queen Helena to face him. Bettie made a sound deep in her throat and stuck so close to me she was practically hiding inside my coat-pocket. Taffy stamped up to me, planted his expensively tailored bulk in front of me, paused a moment to get his breath back after his exertions, and then ignored me to scowl at Queen Helena and the Exiles.

"Why are you talking with these has-beens?" he growled to me. "You know where the real power is in the Nightside. Why didn't you come and talk to me?"

"I don't really want to talk to anyone," I said wistfully. "I keep telling everyone I'm busy right now, but . . ."

"Whatever they've offered you, I'll double it," said Taffy. "And unlike them, you can be sure I'll deliver. I want you on my side, Taylor, and I always get what I want."

"I suggest you take this up with Helena," I said. "She seems to believe she has exclusive rights to me. And you wouldn't believe some of the nasty things she's been saying about you."

And then all I had to do was step quickly to one side, as Uptown Taffy Lewis lurched forward to confront Queen Helena, screaming insults into her cold and unyielding face. She hissed insults right back at him, then the Exiles got involved with Taffy's lieutenants, and suddenly both armies were going for each other's throats. I had already retreated to a safe distance, hauling Bettie along with me, and we watched fascinated as open warfare broke out right in front of us. The tourists loved it, watching it all from a safe distance, and even recording it so they could enjoy it again later.

Queen Helena had her implants, the Exiles, and her followers, but Taffy had the numbers. They swarmed all over Queen Helena and her people, dragging them down despite their elite weapons. I saw Zog thrown to the ground and trampled underfoot, and Tobermoret beaten down with his own staff till it broke. Xerxes was cut open with his own daggers. Helena and Artur stood back to back, killing everyone who came within reach until finally the odds were too great; and then the pair of them disappeared in a sudden blaze of light, leaving the two armies to fight it out in the street. The bodies piled up, and blood flowed thickly in the gutters.

Politics is never dull in the Nightside.

I started off down a side street, leaving the violence behind. Bettie trotted along beside me, still staring back over her shoulder.

"Is that it?" she said. "Aren't you going to do anything?"

"Haven't I done enough?" I said. "By the time they're finished with each other, the two most dangerous armed forces in the Nightside will have wiped each other out. What more do you want?"

"Well, I thought . . . I expected . . ."

"What?"

"I don't know! Something more . . . dramatic! You're the great John Taylor! I thought I was going to see you in action, at last."

"Action is overrated," I said. "Winning is all that matters. Aren't you getting enough good material for your story?"

"Well, yes, but . . . it's not quite what I expected. You're not what I expected." She looked at me thoughtfully. "You faced down Queen Helena and the Exiles, and their army. Told them to go to Hell and damned them to do their worst. And they all backed down. Were you bluffing?"

I grinned. "I'll never tell."

Bettie laughed out loud. "This story is going to make my name! My day on the streets with John Taylor!"

She grabbed me by the shoulders, turned me round, and kissed me hard on the lips. It was an impulse moment. A happy thing. Could have meant anything, or nothing. We stood together a moment, and then she pulled back a little and looked at me with wide, questioning eyes. I could have pushed her away. Could have defused the moment, with a smile or a joke. But I didn't. I pulled her to me and kissed her. Because I wanted to. She filled my arms. We kissed the breath out of each other, while our hands moved up and down each other's bodies. Finally, we broke off, and looked at each other again. Her face was very close, her hurried breath beating against my face. Her face was flushed, her eyes very bright. My head was full of her perfume, and of her. I could feel her heart racing, so close to mine. I could feel the whole length of her body, pressing insistently against mine.

"Well," she said. "I didn't expect that. Has it really been such a long time since you kissed anyone? Since you . . . ?"

I pushed her gently away, and she let me. But her eyes still held mine.

"I can't do this," I said. My voice didn't sound like mine. Didn't sound like someone in control of himself.

"It's true what they say about Suzie, then," said Bettie. She sounded kind, not judgemental. "She can't . . . The poor dear. And poor you, John. That's no way to live. You can't have a real relationship with someone if you can't ever touch her."

"I love her," I said. "She loves me."

"That's not love," said Bettie. "That's one damaged soul clinging to another, for comfort. I could love you, John."

"Of course you could," I said. "You're the daughter of a succubus. Love comes easy to you."

"No," she said. "Just the opposite. I laugh and smile

162

and flutter my eye-lashes because that's what's expected of me. And because it does help, with the job. But that's not me. Or at least, not all of me. I only show that to people I care about. I like you, John. Admire you. I could learn to love you. Could you . . . ?"

"I can't talk about this now," I said.

"You'll have to talk about it sometime. And sometimes . . . you can say things to a stranger that you couldn't say to anyone else."

"You're not a stranger," I said.

"Why thank you, John. That's the nicest thing you've said to me so far."

She moved forward and leaned her head on my shoulder. We held each other gently. No passion, no pressure, only a man and a woman together, and it felt good, so good. It had been a long time since I'd held anyone. Since anyone had held me. It was like . . . part of me had been asleep. Finally, I pushed her away.

"We have to go see the Cardinal," I said firmly. "Pen Donavon and his damned Recording are still out there, somewhere, and that means people like Taffy and Helena will be looking for it, hoping it will turn out to be something they can use to further their ambitions. I really don't like the way they were willing to flaunt their armies openly in public."

"Walker will do something," said Bettie.

"That's what I'm afraid of," I said.

•　　•　　•

Rick Aday's directions finally brought us to a pokey little shop called The Pink Cockatoo, a single-windowed front, in the middle of a long terrace of shops, set between a Used Grimoires book-shop, and a Long Pig franchise. The window before us was full of fashionable fetish clothing that seemed to consist mostly of plastic and leather straps. A few corsets and basques, and some high-heeled boots that would have been too big even for me. Incense candles, fluffy handcuffs, and something with spikes that I preferred not to look at too closely. I tried the door, but it was locked. There was a rusty steel intercom set into the wooden frame. I hit the button with my fist and leaned in close.

"This is John Taylor, to see the Cardinal. Open up, or I'll huff and I'll puff and I'll blow your door right off its hinges."

"This establishment is protected," said a calm, cultured voice. "Even from people like the infamous John Taylor. Now go away, or I'll set the hell-hounds on you."

"We need to talk, Cardinal."

"Convince me."

"I've just been with the Collector," I said. "Discussing the missing Afterlife Recording. He didn't have it. Now either you agree to talk to me, or I'll tell him you've got it and exactly where to find you. And you know how much he's always wanted to make your collection part of his own."

"Bully," the voice said dispassionately. "All right; I

suppose you'd better come in. Bring the demon floozy with you."

There was the sound of several locks and bolts disengaging, and then the door slowly swung open before us. I marched straight in, followed by Bettie. There might have been booby-traps, trap-doors, or all kinds of unpleasantness ahead, but in the Nightside you can't ever afford to look weak. Confidence is everything. The door shut and locked itself behind us. Not entirely to my surprise, the interior of the shop wasn't at all what its exterior had suggested. For one thing, the interior was a hell of a lot bigger. It's a common enough spell in the Nightside, sticking a large space inside a small one, given that living and business space are both in such short supply. The problem lies with the spell, often laid down in a hurry by dodgy backstreet sorcerers, the kind who deal strictly in cash. All it takes is one mistake in the set-up, one mispronunciation of a vital word; and then the whole spell can collapse at any time without any warning. The interior expands suddenly to its full size, shouldering everything else out of the way . . . and they'll be pulling body parts out of the rubble that used to be a street for days on end.

The shop's interior stretched away before me, warmly lit and widely spacious, with gleaming wood-panelled walls, and a spotless floor. The huge barnlike structure was filled with miles and miles of open glass shelving and stands, showing off hundreds of weird and wonderful treasures. Bettie made excited *Ooh!* and *Aah!* noises, and I had to physically prevent her from picking things up to examine them. The Cardinal had said his place was protected, and I believed him. Because if it wasn't seriously protected, the Collector would have cleaned him out by now.

The Cardinal came strolling down the brightly lit central aisle to greet us. A tall and well-proportioned man in his late forties, with a high-boned face, an easy smile, and a hint of mascara round the eyes. He was wearing skintight white slacks, a red shirt open to the navel to show off his shaven chest, and a patterned silk scarf gathered loosely round his neck. He carried a martini in one hand and didn't offer the other to be shaken.

"Wow," I said. "When the Church defrocked you, they went all the way, didn't they?"

The Cardinal smiled easily. "The Church has never approved of those of my . . . inclination. Even though we are responsible for most of the glorious works of art adorning their greatest churches and cathedrals. They only put up with me for so long because I was useful, and a respected academic, and . . . discreet. None of which did me any good when I was found out, and accused . . . It's not as if I took anything important, or significant. I simply wanted a few pretty things for my own. Ah, well; at least I don't have to wear those awful robes any more. So drab, and so very draughty round the nether regions."

"Excuse me," said Bettie, "But why is your shop called The Pink Cockatoo? What has that got to do with . . . well, anything?"

The Cardinal's smile widened. "My little joke. It's called that because I've had a cockatoo in my time."

Bettie got the giggles. I gave the Cardinal my best *Let's try and stick to the subject* look.

"Come to take a look at my collection, have you?" he said, apparently unmoved by the look. He sipped delicately at his martini, one finger elegantly extended. "By all means. Knock yourself out."

I wandered down the shelves, just to be polite. And because I was a bit curious. I kept Bettie close beside me and made sure she maintained a respectful distance from the exhibits at all times. I was sure that the Cardinal believed in *You broke it, you paid for it.* He wandered along behind us, being obviously patient. I recognised some of the things on the shelves, by reputation if not always by sight. The Cardinal had helpfully labelled them in neat copperplate handwriting. There was a copy of the Gospel According to Mary Magdalene. (With illustrations. And I was pretty sure which kind, too.) Pope Joan's robes of office. The rope Judas Iscariot used to hang himself. Half a dozen large canvasses by acknowledged Masters, all unknown to modern art history, depicting frankly pornographic scenes from some of the seamier tales in the Old Testament. Probably private commissions, from aristocratic patrons of the time. A Satanic Bible, bound in black goat's skin, with an inverted crucifix stamped in bas-relief on the front cover.

"Now that's a very limited edition," said the Cardinal, leaning in close to peer over my shoulder. "Belonged to

Giles de Rais, the old monster himself, before he met the Maid of Orleans. There are only seventeen copies of that particular edition, in the goat's skin."

"Why seventeen?" said Bettie. "Bit of an arbitrary number, isn't it?"

"I said that," said the Cardinal. "When I inquired further, I was told that seventeen is the most you can get out of one goat's skin. Makes you wonder whether the last copy had a big floppy ear hanging off the back cover . . . And I hate to think what they used for the spine. Ah, Mr. Taylor, I see you've discovered my dice. I'm rather proud of those. The very dice the Roman soldiers used as they gambled for the Christ's clothes, while he was still on the cross."

"Do they have any . . . special properties?" I said, moving in close for a better look. They seemed very ordinary, two small wooden cubes, with any colour and all the dots worn away long ago.

"No," said the Cardinal. "They're just dice. Their value, which is incredible, lies in their history."

"And what's *this*?" said Bettie, wrinkling her nose as she studied a single, small, very old and apparently very ordinary fish, enclosed in a clear Lucite block.

"Ah, that," said the Cardinal. "The only surviving example of the fish used to feed the five thousand . . . You wouldn't believe how much money, political positions, and even sexual favours I've been offered, by certain extreme epicures, just for a taste . . . The philistines."

"What brought you here, to the Nightside, Cardinal?"

said Bettie, doing her best to sound pleasant and casual and not at all like a reporter. The Cardinal wasn't fooled, but he smiled indulgently, and she hurried on. "And why collect only Christian artifacts? Are you still a believer, even after everything the Church has done to you?"

"Of course," said the Cardinal. "The Catholic Church is not unlike the Mafia, in some ways—once in, never out. And as for the Nightside—why this is Hell, nor am I out of it. Ah, the old jokes are still the best. I damned myself to this appalling haven for the morally intransigent through the sin of greed, of acquisition. I was tempted, and I fell. Sometimes it feels like I'm still falling . . . but I have my collection to comfort me." He drained the last of his martini, smacked his lips, put the glass down carefully next to a miniature golden calf, and looked at me steadily. "Why are you here, Mr. Taylor? What do you want with me? You must know I can't trust you. Not after you worked for the Vatican, finding the Unholy Grail for them."

"I worked for a particular individual," I said carefully. "Not the Vatican, as such."

"You really did find it, didn't you?" said the Cardinal, looking at me almost wistfully. I could all but sense his collector's fingers twitching. "The Sombre Cup . . . What was it like?"

"There aren't the words," I said. "But don't bother trying to track it down. It's been . . . defused. It's only a cup now."

"It's still history," said the Cardinal.

Bettie stooped suddenly, to pick up an open paperback from a chair. "*The Da Vinci Code*? Are you actually reading this, Cardinal?"

"Oh, yes . . . I love a good laugh."

"Put it down, Bettie," I said. "It'll probably turn out to be some exotic misprinting, and he'll charge us for getting fingerprints all over it. Cardinal, we're here about the Afterlife Recording. I take it you have heard of Pen Donavon's DVD?"

"Of course. But . . . I have decided I'm not interested in pursuing it. I don't want it. Because I know myself. I know it wouldn't be enough for me simply to possess the DVD. I'd have to watch it . . . And I don't think I'm ready to see what's on it."

"You think it might test your faith?" I said.

"Perhaps . . ."

"Aren't you curious?" said Bettie.

"Of course . . . But it's one thing to believe, another to know. I do try to hope for the best, but when the Holy Father himself has told you to your face that you're damned for all time, just for being what God made you . . . Hope is all I have left. It's not much of a substitute for faith, but even cold comfort is better than none."

"I believe God has more mercy than that," I said. "I don't think God sweats the small stuff."

"Yes, well," said the Cardinal dryly, "you'd have to believe that, wouldn't you?"

"If you learn anything, let me know," I said. "As long as the Afterlife Recording is out there, loose in the wind, more people will be trying to get their hands on it, for all the wrong reasons. There's even a chance the Removal Man is interested in it."

All the colour dropped out of the Cardinal's face, his brittle amiability replaced by stark terror. "He can't come here! He can't! Have you seen him? You could have led him here! To me! No, no, no . . . You have to leave. Right now. I can't take the risk!"

And he pushed both Bettie and me towards the door. He wasn't big enough to budge either of us if we didn't want to be budged, but I didn't see any point in making a scene. He didn't know anything useful. So I let him shove and propel us back to the door and push us through it. Once we were back on the street, the door slammed shut behind us, and a whole series of locks and bolts snapped into place. It seemed the Cardinal believed in traditional ways of protecting himself, too. I adjusted my trench coat. It had been a long time since I'd been given the bum's rush. And then from behind the door came a scream, loud and piercing, a harsh shrill sound full of abject terror. I beat on the door, and yelled into the intercom, but the scream went on and on and on, long after human lungs should have been unable to sustain it. The pain and horror in the sound was almost unbearable. And then it stopped, abruptly, and that was worse.

The locks and the bolts slowly opened, one at a time, and the door swung inwards. I made Bettie stand behind me and pushed the door all the way open. Beyond it, I could see the huge display room. No sign of anyone, anywhere. No sound at all. I moved slowly, and very cautiously forward, refusing to allow Bettie to hurry me. There was no sign of the Cardinal anywhere. And every single piece of his collection was gone, too. Nothing left but empty shelves, stretching away.

"The Removal Man," I said. My voice echoed on the quiet, saying the name over and over again.

"Did we lead him here, do you think?" said Bettie, her voice hushed. The echo turned her words into disturbing whispers.

"No," I said. "I'd have known if anyone was following us. I'm sure I'd have known."

"Even the Removal Man? Even him?"

"Especially him," I said.

# SEVEN

*The Good, the Bad, and the Ungodly*

"So," said Bettie Divine, sitting perched on one of the empty wooden shelves with her long legs dangling, "what do we do now? I mean, the Removal Man has just removed our last real lead. Though I have to say . . . I never thought I'd get this close to him. The Removal Man is a *real* urban legend. Even more than you, darling. We're talking about someone who actually does move in mysterious ways! Maybe I should forget this story and concentrate on him. If I could bring in an exclusive interview with the Removal Man . . ."

"You mean you're giving up on me?" I said, more amused than anything.

Bettie shrugged easily. She was now wearing a pale

blue cat-suit, with a long silver zip running from collar to crotch. Her hair was bobbed, and her horns peeped out from under a smart peaked cap. "Well, I am half demon, darling; you have to expect the odd moment of heartlessness."

"If you stick with me, at least there's a reasonable chance you'll survive to file your story," I said.

"Who'd want to hurt a poor sweet defenceless little girlie like me?" said Bettie, pouting provocatively. "And besides, we half demons are notoriously hard to kill. That's why the Editor paired me up with you for this story. Which, you have to admit, does seem to have petered out rather. I mean to say, if the Collector doesn't have the Afterlife Recording, and the Cardinal doesn't have it, who does that leave?"

"There are others," I said. "Strange Harald, the junkman. Flotsam Inc.; their motto: *We buy and sell anything that isn't actually nailed down and guarded by hellhounds*. And there's always Bishop Beastly . . . But admittedly they're all fairly minor players. Far too small to think they could handle a prize like the Afterlife Recording. They'd have sold it on immediately; and I would have heard. You know, it's always possible Pen Donavon could have realised how much trouble he'd let himself in for and destroyed the DVD."

"He'd better not have!" said Bettie, her eyes flashing dangerously. "The paper owns that DVD, no matter what's on it."

I looked at her thoughtfully. "If it is real . . . are you curious to see what's on it?"

"Of course," she said immediately. "I want to know. I always want to know."

"So you'll stick with me? Until we find it?"

"Of course, darling! Forget about the Removal Man. It was just an impulse. No; we're on the trail of something that could shake the whole Nightside if it is real. And you know what that means? I could end up covering a real story at last! Do you know how long I've dreamed about covering a real story, about something that actually matters? We can't let this end here! You're the private eye, you're the legendary John Taylor; do something!"

"I'm open to suggestions," I said.

My mobile phone rang. I answered and was immediately assaulted by the acerbic voice of Alex Morrisey, calling from Strangefellows. As always, Alex did not sound at all happy with the world, the universe, and everything.

"Taylor, get your arse over here at warp factor ten. A certain Pen Donavon has just turned up in my bar, looking like death warmed over and allowed to congeal. He's clutching a DVD case like it's his last life-line, hyperventilating, and crying his eyes out because he thinks the Removal Man is after him. He appears to be suffering from the sad delusion that you can protect him. He says you're the only person he can trust, which only goes to show he doesn't know you very well. So will you please come and get him because he is scaring off all my customers! Most of whom have understandably decided that they don't want to get caught in the inevitable cross-fire. Did I mention that I am not at all happy about this? You are costing me a whole night's profits!"

"Put it on my tab," I said. "I can cover it; I'm on expenses. Sit on Donavon till I get there. No-one talks to him but me."

I put the phone away and smiled at Bettie. "We're back in the game. Pen Donavon has turned up at Strangefellows."

Bettie clapped her hands together, kicked her heels, and jumped down from the wooden shelf. "I knew you'd find him, John! Never doubted you for a moment! And we're finally going to Strangefellows! Super cool!"

"You'll probably be disappointed," I said. "It's only a bar."

"The oldest bar in the world! Where all the customers are myths and legends, and the fate of the whole world gets decided on a regular basis!"

"Only sometimes," I said.

"Is it far from here?"

"Right on the other side of town. Fortunately, I know a short cut."

I took out my Strangefellows club membership card. Alex handed out a dozen or so, in a rare generous moment, and he's been trying to get them back ever since. Not that any of us are ever likely to give them up. They're far too useful. The card itself isn't much to look at. Just simple embossed pasteboard, with the name of the bar in dark Gothic script, and below that the words

*You Are Here*, in blood-red lettering. I pulled Bettie in close beside me, and she snuggled up companionably. I still wasn't used to that. It had been a long time since I'd let anybody get this close to me. This casual. I liked it. I pressed my thumb firmly against the crimson lettering on the card, and it activated at once, throbbing and pulsing with stored energy. It leapt out of my hand to hang on the air before me, turning end over end and crackling with arcane activity. Bright lights flared and sputtered all around it. Alex had paid for the full bells and whistles package. The card expanded suddenly to the size of a door, which opened before us. Together, Bettie and I stepped through into Strangefellows, and the door slammed shut behind us.

I put the card back in my coat-pocket and looked around. The place was unnaturally still and quiet, empty apart from a single drunk sleeping one off, slumped forward across his table. I knew him vaguely. Thallassa, a wizened old sorcerer who claimed to be responsible for the sinking of Atlantis. He said he drank to forget, but it was amazing how many stories he could remember, as long as you were dumb enough to keep buying him drinks. Everyone else had clearly decided that discretion was the better part of running for the hills, and that the combination of Pen Donavon, his DVD, and me in one place was just too dangerous to be around. Even the kind of people who habitually drink at a place like Strangefellows have their limit; and I'm often it.

Donavon was easy to spot. He was sitting slumped on a stool at the bar. No-one else could look that miserable, beaten down, and shit scared from the back. He peered round as Bettie and I approached, and almost collapsed off his stool before he recognised me. He was just a small, ordinary-looking man, no-one you'd look at twice in the street, clearly in way over his head and going down for the third time. Up close, he looked in pretty bad shape. He was shaking and shivering, his face drawn and ashen, with dark circles under his eyes as though he hadn't slept in days. Perhaps because he didn't dare. He couldn't have been half-way through his twenties, but now he looked twice that. Something had aged him and hadn't been kind about it. He clutched a long, shabby coat around him, as though to keep out a chill only he could feel.

He looked like a man who'd seen Hell. Or Heaven.

Alex Morrisey glared at me, and then went back to half-coaxing, half-bullying Donavon into putting aside his brandy glass and trying some freshly made hot soup. Donavon remained unconvinced. He watched, wide-eyed, until Bettie and I were right there with him. Then he sighed deeply, and some of the tension seemed to go out of him. He emptied his glass with a gulp and signalled for another. Alex put aside the soup bowl, sniffed loudly, and reluctantly opened a new bottle.

Alex owns and runs Strangefellows, and possibly as a result, has a mad on for the whole world. He loathes his customers, despises tourists, and never gives the right change on principle. He also had his thirtieth birthday just the other day, which hadn't helped. He always wore black, because, he said, he was in mourning for his sex life. (Gone, but not forgotten.) His permanent scowl had etched a deep notch between his eyebrows, right above the designer shades he always affected. He also wore a snazzy black beret, perched far back on his head to hide his spreading bald patch. I have known clinically depressed lepers with haemorrhoids who smiled more often than Alex Morrisey. Though at least he doesn't have to worry when he sneezes. I leaned against the bar and looked at him reproachfully.

"You never made me hot soup, Alex."

He sniffed loudly. "My home-made soup is full of things that are good for you, including a few that are downright healthful, all of which would be wasted on a body as ruined and ravaged as yours."

"Just because I don't like vegetables . . ."

"You're the only man I know who makes the sign of the cross when confronted with broccoli. And don't change the subject! Once again I am left clearing up the mess from one of your cases. Like I don't have enough troubles of my own. Bloody eels have got into the beer barrels again, the pixies have been at the bar snacks, which they will live to regret, the poor fools, and my pet vulture is pregnant! Someone's going to pay for this . . ."

He broke off as Pen Donavon suddenly reached out and grabbed my arm. There was so little strength left in him it felt like a ghost tugging at my sleeve. His mouth worked for a moment before easing into something like a smile, and there were real tears of gratitude in his eyes.

"Thank God you're here, Mr. Taylor. I've been so afraid . . . They're after me. Everyone's after me. You have to protect me!"

"Of course, of course I will," I said soothingly. "You're safe now. No-one's going to get to you here."

"Just keep them away," he said pathetically. "Keep them all away. I can't think . . . I've been running from everyone. Either they want to pressure me into selling the Recording, or they want to kill me and take it. I can't trust anyone any more. I thought I'd be safe, once I'd made my deal with the *Unnatural Inquirer*, but I was ambushed on my way there. I've been running and hiding ever since."

He let go of me and looked back at the full glass of brandy before him. He gulped half of it down in one go, and Alex winced visibly. Must have been the really good stuff, then. I looked at Bettie.

"Could someone in your offices have put the word out on Donavon coming in with the DVD?"

"For a percentage? Wouldn't surprise me. None of us are exactly overpaid at the *Inquirer*. And our Reception phones are always being tapped. We debug them at the start of every working day, but there's always someone listening in, hoping for an advantage. After all, we hear everything first. We're noted for it."

"I should never have recorded the broadcast," said

Donavon. He was sitting hunched over his brandy glass, as though afraid someone would snatch it away. "It was all a ghastly mistake. I was trying to contact the other side, yes, but I never thought . . . My life hasn't been my own since. And I'd certainly never have tried to sell the Recording if I'd known it would destroy my whole life."

"You saw the broadcast," said Bettie, leaning in close with her best engaging smile. "What did you see?"

Donavon started shaking again. He tried to speak, and couldn't. He squeezed his eyes shut, and tears ran down his trembling cheeks. Alex sighed heavily and topped up the brandy glass again. He smiled nastily at me.

"All these drinks are going on your tab, Taylor."

I smiled right back at him. "Do your worst. Expenses, remember?"

"Well," said Bettie. "You will get expenses if we deliver the DVD."

I looked at her. "What? What do you mean *if*? Nothing was ever said about my expenses being conditional!"

"This is the newspaper game, sweetie. Everything's conditional."

I scowled, and then had to stop because it was upsetting Donavon even more. I moved away down the bar and gestured for Alex to lean in close. "You can bet some of your recent customers will be out on the streets now, spilling the beans about who and what can be found in Strangefellows. Which means we can expect unfriendly visitors at any moment. Better lock the doors and slam down the shutters. Where are the Coltranes?"

"Out the back, doing exactly that," said Alex. "I can think for myself, thank you. My defences will keep out all but the most determined; but if anyone does get in, the resulting damage will also be going on your tab. I'd insure against you, but apparently you're classed along with Acts of Gods and other unavoidable nuisances."

"Call Suzie," I said. "I think we're going to need her help on this one."

"Damn," said Alex. "And I just had the place redecorated."

Bettie slipped her arm through mine and turned me round to face her. "I hate to sound disappointed," she said, "but I am, maybe a bit. I mean, darling, this isn't at all what I expected. It all looks so . . . ordinary. Well, ordinary for the Nightside. I was hoping for something more . . . extreme."

I refrained from pointing out the disembodied hand scuttling up and down the bar top. (Alex accepted it in payment for a bad debt.) The hand was busy polishing the bar top and refilling the snack bowls. Yet another good reason not to eat them, as far as I was concerned. Alex objected on principle to giving away anything, and it showed in his choice of snacks. Does anyone actually eat honeyed locusts any more? The vulture's perch was empty, of course, but there were other things to look at. Lightning, crackling inside a bottle. Bit hard on the ship, I thought. A small featureless furry thing, that sat on the bar top purring happily to itself, and occasionally farting. Until the hand grabbed it up and used it as a rag to polish the bar top. A small cuspidor of tanna leaves, with the brand-name *Mummy's favourite*. All nice homey touches.

"I want a drink," Bettie announced loudly. "I want one of those special drinkies you can only get here. Do you have a Maiden's Bloody Ruin? Dragons' Breath? Angel's Tears?"

"The first two aren't cocktails," I said. "And that last one is actually called Angel's Urine."

"Which was selling quite well," said Alex. "Until word got around it wasn't so much a trade name as an accurate description."

Bettie laughed and snuggled cosily up against me. "You choose, darling."

"Give the lady a wormwood brandy," I said.

Alex gave me a look, and then fished about under the bar for the really good stuff he keeps set aside for special customers.

"I do like this place, after all," Bettie decided. "It's cosy, and comfortable. It'd probably even have atmosphere if there was anybody else here but us. Ah, sweetie, you take me to the nicest places!"

She kissed me. As though it was the most natural thing in the world. Perhaps it was, for other people. I took her in my arms, and her whole body surged forward, pressing against me. When we broke apart, Alex was there, pushing a glass of wormwood brandy towards Bettie. She snatched it up with an excited squeak, sipped the brandy, and made appreciative noises. Alex looked at me. I looked at him. Neither of us mentioned Suzie, but we were both thinking about her.

And then we all looked round sharply at the sound of heavy footsteps in the entrance lobby upstairs. They were heading our way, and they didn't sound like customers. Alex cursed dispassionately.

"My defences are telling me that a bunch of combat sorcerers just walked right through them, without even hesitating. Really powerful combat sorcerers."

"How can you tell?" said Bettie

"Because only really powerful combat sorcerers could get through this bar's defences," I said.

Thirteen very dangerous men came clattering down the metal stairs into the bar proper, making a hell of a racket in the process. They moved smoothly, in close formation, and spread out at the bottom of the steps to cut us off from all the exits. They stood tall and proud, radiating professionalism and confidence. They were all dressed in black leather cowboy outfits, complete with Stetsons, chaps, boots, and silver spurs. Surprisingly, and a bit worryingly, they weren't wearing holsters. They all possessed various charms, amulets, fetishes, and grisgris, displayed openly around their necks or on their chests for all to see, and despair. These were major league power sources, for strength and speed, transformations and elemental commands. A bit generic but no less dangerous for that.

They all looked to be big men and in their prime. They all had that lazy arrogance that comes from having beaten down anyone and anything that ever dared to stand against them. You don't get to be a combat sorcerer without killing an awful lot of people in the process. There was an ideogram tattooed on all their foreheads, right over the third eye, showing their Clan affiliation. Combat sorcerers are too dangerous to be allowed to run around unsupervised. You either joined a Clan, or they joined together to wipe you out. This particular bunch belonged to Clan Buckaroo.

Their leader stepped forward to face me. He was a good head taller than me, broad in the shoulders and narrow in the waist. Probably ate his vegetables every day, and did a hundred and fifty sit-ups before breakfast. He had three different charms hanging from rolled silver chains around his neck and an amulet round his waist I didn't like to look at. This cowboy was packing some serious firepower. He fixed me with his cold blue eyes and started to say something that would only have been an insult or a demand, and I wasn't in the mood for either; so I got my retaliation in first.

"Those are seriously tacky outfits," I said. "What are you planning to do, line dance us to death?"

The leader hesitated. This wasn't going according to plan. He wasn't used to defiance, let alone open ridicule. He squared his shoulders and tried again.

"We are Clan Buckaroo. We work for Kid Cthulhu. And you've got something we want."

"Like what?" I asked. "Fashion sense?"

The leader's hand dropped to where his holster should

have been. The twelve other combat sorcerers all did the same. Some suddenly had guns of light in their hands, sparking and shimmering. Like the ghosts of guns steeped in slaughter. And a few, including the leader, just pointed their index fingers at me, like a child miming a gun. I looked at the leader and raised an eyebrow.

"Conceptual guns," he said. "Creations of the mind, powered by murder magic. They never miss, they never run out of ammunition, they can punch a hole through anything; and they kill whatever they hit. Allow me to demonstrate."

He pointed his finger at the bottles ranked behind the bar. I grabbed Bettie and Donavon and dragged them out of the way. One by one the bottles exploded, showering glass fragments and hissing liquids all over the bar. Alex stood his ground and didn't move an inch, even as liquors soaked his shirt, and flying glass cut his cheek. The leader raised his finger to his lips and blew away imaginary smoke. The disembodied hand flipped him the finger, and then disappeared under the bar. The watching cowboys were all grinning broadly. Alex glared right back at them.

"You needn't be so smug. You only got the stuff I keep for tourists. The good stuff can look after itself."

The leader looked at him for a moment. He'd used his favourite trick, and no-one was looking the least bit intimidated. He stuck out his chin and tried again.

"I've come for the Afterlife Recording."

"Don't worry, dear," said Bettie. "I'm sure you were just a bit over-excited."

I stepped forward, putting myself between her and the leader. I looked him square in the eye. "You don't want to be here," I said. "These aren't the people you're looking for."

I held his gaze with mine, and he stood very still. Behind him, the other combat sorcerers stirred restlessly. And then the leader smiled coldly right back at me.

"I've heard about your evil eye, Taylor. Won't work on any of us. We're protected."

He was right. I couldn't stare him down, couldn't even reach him. While I was still working out what to do next, Bettie stepped past me and put herself between me and the leader.

"Trevor!" she said. "I thought it was you, sweetie! Didn't recognise you at first, all tricked out in the Village People outfit. You never told me you were a combat sorcerer."

The other cowboys looked at their leader, and I could practically see them mouthing the word *Trevor?* at each other. The leader glared at Bettie.

"That is my old name," he said harshly. "I don't use it any more. My name is Ace now, Bettie, leader of Clan Buckaroo. I haven't gone by . . . that other name in ages."

"You were Trevor when I knew you," Bettie said briskly. "I did wonder why you insisted on wearing those black boots and spurs to bed, but I thought you were being kinky. Even though you went all bashful when I got out the fluffy handcuffs. What are you doing here, sweetie, dressed up as Black Bart and leading this bunch of overdressed thugs?"

"The money's good," said Ace.

"It would have to be," said Bettie.

"Don't get in the way," said Ace, giving her his best fierce glare. "We're here to do a job, and we're going to do it. I can't cut you any slack just because we used to be an item."

"You and he were an item?" I said to Bettie.

She shrugged. "He didn't last long."

There was some quiet sniggering from the other combat sorcerers that died quickly away as Ace glared around him.

"What exactly are you here for?" I said. "Maybe there's room for negotiation."

"We want Donavon, and we want the Afterlife Recording," said Ace, fixing me with his cold stare again. "No negotiations, no discussion. We work for Kid Cthulhu, and he wants sole ownership of the Recording."

"Now wait just a minute!" Bettie strode forward to glare right into Ace's face, and he was so startled he actually fell back a pace. "The *Unnatural Inquirer* has already purchased exclusive rights to all the material on that DVD! We have a binding contract! We own it!"

"Not any more you don't," said Ace. "Possession is everything, in the Nightside."

"Kid Cthulhu . . ." Alex said thoughtfully. "Thought I'd heard something about his having cash liquidity problems with his undersea-farming interests. And, of course, the bottom's dropped right out of the calamari market. He must be thinking he can make enough money out of the Afterlife Recording to bail him out. So to speak."

"You can't have the Afterlife Recording!" Bettie said firmly to Ace. "We got there first."

Ace looked at the cowboy next to him. "If she speaks again, kill her."

Bettie's mouth opened wide, outraged, and I clapped a hand across it and hauled her back. Ace didn't look like he was kidding to me. Thirteen combat sorcerers in one room can do pretty much whatever they feel like doing. But, on the other hand, I had a reputation to maintain . . . So I looked Alex in the eye and gave him my best disapproving stare.

"Now that was just plain rude," I said. "And if you threaten to kill me . . . I will smite the lot of you. Right here and now."

There was a pause, and the thirteen combat sorcerers looked at me uncertainly. With anyone else, they'd have dismissed it immediately as just talk. But I was John Taylor . . .

"Bettie Divine is under my protection," I said. "Along with everyone else in this bar. Very definitely including Pen Donavon. So you can all get your redneck wannabe big bad selves out of here, before I decide to do something quite appallingly nasty to you."

The combat sorcerers looked at each other, and then at their leader. Their magical guns or fingers were all pointing at the floor. And then Ace smiled at me and laughed softly, and just like that the mood was broken.

"Never make a threat you can't back up," he said.

Ace pointed his conceptual gun at the drunk sorcerer, still out cold despite all the drama going on around him. A tired old man, who might or might not have done a terrible thing in his younger days. Ace shot him three times, his pointed finger unwavering even as the invisible bullets punched large bloody holes in the sleeping man. Thallassa's body jumped and jerked under the impact of the bullets, but he never made a sound. He just lay where he was, slumped across his table, as the blood ran out of him. Murdered, for no reason he would ever know. Ace laughed briefly and turned back to me.

"Boys," he said, "kill everyone in this place except for Pen Donavon." He smiled at Bettie. "Sorry, sweetie. Just business. You know how it is."

"You little shit," Bettie said defiantly. "And I do mean *little*, Trevor. I've had more fun with a toothpick."

Women always fight dirty.

Ace pointed his finger at her. "Shut up and die, will you?"

"Not in my bar," said Alex. He produced a pump-action shotgun from under the bar, and when Ace turned to look, Alex shot him in the face. Ace was thrown backwards, blasted right off his feet, crashing into the cowboys behind him, who made shocked, startled noises. Alex worked the pump action, and all the combat sorcerers stood very still.

"Wow," I said. "Hard core, Alex."

He shrugged modestly. "Suzie left this behind, one night. Always thought it would come in handy one day. I loaded it with silver bullets, dipped in holy water, and blessed by a wandering god. I could shoot the head off a golem with this. And if golems had other things, I could shoot them off, too."

"You know," said Bettie, "I think I'd be rather more impressed if Trevor wasn't getting up again."

We looked round. Ace was already back on his feet, apparently entirely unaffected. Apart from the really pissed-off look on his face.

"Oh, shit," said Alex, putting down the shotgun. "Guys, you're on your own. If you want me, I'll be hiding behind the bar, whimpering and wetting myself."

"Really?" said Bettie, not bothering to hide her disappointment in him.

"Hell no," said Alex. "This is my bar! It's bad enough that the whole world conspires against me, messes with my beer and puts my vulture up the duff, without having a bunch of refugees from an S&M march walking in here like they own the place. And Thallassa hadn't even paid for his drinks yet, you bastards! You owe me money!" He vaulted over the bar, holding a glowing cricket bat. "Merlin made this for me, sometime back. For when you really, absolutely have to take out the trash."

"Alex," I said. "This isn't like you. It's an improvement, but it isn't like you."

"My new girl-friend's upstairs," said Alex. "Probably

watching on the monitors. You know how it is when you've got a new girl. You end up doing all kinds of stupid things."

"Yes," I said. "I know how it is."

"Is that it?" said Ace, smiling. "A glow-in-the-dark cricket bat?"

"No," said Alex. *"Oh, girls!"*

And Alex's two large, muscular, body-building bouncers, Betty and Lucy Coltrane, came charging in from the back of the bar and threw themselves at the startled combat sorcerers. They ploughed right into the group before the cowboys even had time to react, knocking them arse over tit and kicking them while they were down, in the fine old tradition of bouncers everywhere. Alex hit the group a moment later, swinging his cricket bat with both hands as though it were a long sword. He smashed faces and broke bones, and the cowboys fell back, crying out in shock and distress. None of them had prepared for an irate bartender armed with a weapon enchanted by Merlin Satanspawn. The glowing cricket bat smashed through their magical defences like they weren't even there. Tougher magical shields flared up here and there, as some of the combat sorcerers got their act together enough to ward off the Coltranes, but the girls just dodged around the shields to get at those cowboys who weren't protected. Shrill cries of pain and anguish filled the air.

I said Ace's name, and when he turned to look at me I threw a handful of pepper into his face. An attack so basic and physical his magical shields couldn't do a thing to prevent it. He howled piteously, scrabbling at his tearing eyes with both hands. I kicked him in the nuts, and he folded up and fell to the floor. Top-rank combat sorcerer, my arse. Try having assassins at your throat and at your back ever since you were a small child and see what that does to your survival skills.

Some of the combat sorcerers got past their shock and surprise and charged up their amulets and charms. They fired spells in all directions, and everyone ducked for cover. I looked around for Pen Donavon, just in time to see him diving behind the bar. Best place for him. Then I had to throw myself to one side as an energy bolt seared through the air where I'd been a moment before. It hit the long wooden bar and cracked it from end to end. I winced. I knew I was going to end up paying for that. Betty and Lucy Coltrane were ducking and dodging, avoiding fireballs and transformation spells and conceptual bullets from all directions at once. They were fast on their feet for their size, but they couldn't protect themselves and press the fight at the same time.

Sparks flew from Alex's cricket bat as he clubbed his way through the cowboys before him. They blasted him with destructive spells at point-blank range, but the magic Merlin had built into the bat reflected the spells right back at their source. As a result, lightning bolts flashed back and forth across the bar, bouncing off magical shields and doing extensive damage to the bar's fixtures and fittings. Magical bullets ricocheted, punching holes in the walls and ceiling. And two rather surprised-looking toads blinked at each other from piles of cowboy clothes before reappearing as themselves again.

Meanwhile, I had my own problem. Ace was getting up again. I picked up a handy chair and hit him over the head with it. I'm a great one for tradition. But the chair didn't break, and Ace didn't go down. So much for Hollywood. I dropped the chair and looked around for something else to hit him with. Preferably something with big jaggedy edges. I saw one of the combat sorcerers grab Bettie by the arm and pull her to him. I think he intended to use her as a human shield, or as a way to get to me. He really should have known better. He pointed his shimmering gun at her, and she smiled dazzlingly at him. He hesitated, and was lost. He stood where he was, unmoving, fascinated. Bettie's mother was a lust demon, and had passed on some of her deadly glamour to her daughter. Bettie held the cowboy's eyes with hers, fished in her bag, brought out her Mace, and let him have it. He fell to the floor, writhing and howling, and clawing at his eyes with both hands.

And to think I'd been a bit worried that she might not fit in with my friends.

While I was distracted, Ace hit me with a transformation spell. I cried out in shock as the spell crawled all over me, cramping my muscles and coursing through my neural system. Pain bent me in two, and sweat dripped from my face. I could feel my skin stretching and distorting, trying to find a new shape. Discharging energies spat and crackled around me, but for all its power, the spell couldn't find a foothold in me. Slowly, I straightened up again, fighting back the effects of the spell, throwing it off through sheer force of will. I smiled slowly at Ace, a cold and nasty death's-head grin, and he fell back a pace as the last of his spell fell away from me, defeated.

"So," he said harshly. "It's true. You're not human. That spell would have worked on any man."

"A man might have shown you mercy," I said. "But we're beyond that now."

He thrust his conceptual gun in my face. I grabbed his pointing finger and broke it. And while he was distracted by the pain, I reached automatically for my gift, to find some weakness in his defences . . . and it was there, just waiting to be used. I didn't waste any time wondering why. I simply fired up my gift, reached out with my mind, and found the operating spells controlling the combat sorcerers' magical items. And then it was the easiest thing in the world to tear away all the items' controls and restraints and let the amulets and charms and fetishes release all their power at once.

I could have fixed it so they would discharge harmlessly, but I didn't feel like being merciful.

The magical items exploded like grenades, blowing their owners apart. Thirteen cowboys cried out in shock and pain and horror as their power sources punched holes through their chests, tore off their arms, or blew their heads apart. It was all over in a few moments, and then there were thirteen dead combat sorcerers lying on the bar-room floor, in slowly spreading pools of blood and gore. Alex lowered his glowing cricket bat, breathing hard. Betty and Lucy Coltrane looked around, kicked the bodies nearest them just in case, and then high-fived each other.

Bettie Divine looked at me, shock and horror in her face.

"John; what have you done?"

"He said *Kill them all.*"

"That doesn't mean you had to kill all of them!"

"Yes it did," I said. "I have a reputation to maintain."

*"What?"*

"They threatened me, and my friends, and they killed a poor drunk sorcerer. They broke my first rule. *Thou shalt not mess with me and mine.* I just sent a message to Kid Cthulhu and all his kind."

"You killed thirteen men to make a point?" Bettie was staring at me as though she'd never seen me before, and perhaps she hadn't. Not this me.

"They would have killed you," I said.

"Yes. They would have. But you're supposed to be better than that."

"I am," I said. "Sometimes."

She wasn't even looking at me any more. She knelt beside what was left of the man called Ace. He'd carried three magical charms, and they'd torn him apart as they detonated. The amulet had blown his hand right off his wrist. His head was still pretty much intact. He looked more surprised than anything. Bettie cupped his face with one hand.

"We were close, once. When we were both a lot younger. He wasn't always like this. We had dreams, of all the wonderful things we were going to do. And I became a reporter for a tabloid, and he ended up as a cowboy. He wasn't bad, not when I knew him. He liked silly comedies, and happy endings, and he held me on bad days and told me he believed in me. And yes, I know, he would have killed me if you hadn't stopped me. That doesn't change anything."

"Did you love him?" I said.

"Of course I loved him. The man he was then. But I don't think he'd been that man for some time." She stared down at the dead face, into his staring eyes. She tried to close the eyelids, but they wouldn't stay closed. Bettie made a sound, and sat back on her heels. "I thought I'd be stronger than this. Harder, more cynical. The things I've seen, and done . . . the death of someone who used to be a friend, long ago, shouldn't affect me like this. I didn't think I could still hurt like this."

"You get used to it," I said. And immediately knew it was the wrong thing to say. "Bettie, you've got nothing to feel bad about. This is all down to me."

"Yes," she said. "It is."

She got up, all calm and composed again, and walked straight past me to the bar. She picked up her drink and took a dainty sip. She didn't look at me once. And I knew she'd never look at me the same way again, after seeing what I could do, what I would do, when pushed to the wall.

I will always do whatever is necessary, to protect my friends, whether they approve or not.

Alex helped Betty and Lucy Coltrane loot the bodies of anything worth the having, and then directed them to haul the bodies out back and dump them in the alley outside. Where the Nightside's various scavengers would quickly dispose of them. There's not a lot of room for sentiment in the Nightside. I would have helped, but I was busy thinking. Why had control of my gift been returned to me, after being blocked twice already? Presumably, whoever had been interfering with my gift just didn't need to any more. Because they were watching over me and knew I'd located Pen Donavon.

Still musing, I wandered back to the bar. Alex had finally persuaded Donavon to come out from behind it, and he was emerging slowly, bit by bit, staring with horrified eyes at all the carnage and destruction.

"They'll always be coming after me, won't they?" he said sadly. "It's never going to be over. I'm never going to get my life back. It wasn't much, but it was mine, and it was safe."

"You'll be safe again once we get you and the Afterlife Recording back to the *Unnatural Inquirer*'s offices," Bettie said briskly. "You'll have the paper's full resources behind you. No-one will dare touch you."

"And once you've handed over the DVD, no-one will have any reason to go after you," I said.

"They might expect me to intercept another broadcast," said Donavon.

"We've seen your television," I said. "Smash it. End of problem."

"We'll never make it to the paper's offices," said Donavon. "They'll be lining up to get at me, all along the way."

"John will find a way," Alex said firmly. "It's what he does. When he isn't busy trashing my bar."

"He doesn't have his gift any more," said Bettie. "He's been neutered."

"Actually, no," I said. "I've got it back, now I've caught up with Donavon. Tell me, Pen, what made you think to come here, looking for me?"

"I got a phone call," said Donavon. "It said I'd be safe at Strangefellows. That John Taylor could protect me. I knew your name, of course. And the bar's reputation."

"Who called you?" I said.

"Don't know. Identity withheld. I didn't recognise the voice. But I was desperate, so . . ."

Alex looked at me. "Kid Cthulhu?"

"Maybe," I said. "Or maybe there's another player in this game. Someone powerful enough to shut down my gift until it didn't matter any more. And just maybe, someone who wanted me to find Donavon, eventually . . . The rules of this game seem to be changing. I wonder why."

"I'd better track down Suzie," said Alex.

"She might have her phone turned off if she's busy. You know Suzie's only really happy when she's working. If you can find her, tell her I need her the moment she's free. I've got a feeling this case is going to get seriously ugly."

"Got it," said Alex. He turned away to root through the mess at the back of the bar, searching through the debris for his phone.

Bettie was looking at me now, her expression hard to read. I looked patiently back, waiting for her to make the first move.

"Is that what you and Suzie have in common?" she said finally. "The thing that holds you together? That you're both killers?"

"It's not that simple," I said.

"I've never understood what you see in Shotgun Suzie. She's a monster. She lives to kill. How can you stay with someone like that?"

"No-one else has shared what we've shared," I said. "Seen the things we've seen, done the things we've had to do. There's no-one else we could talk to, no-one else who'd understand."

"I want to understand," said Bettie. She moved slowly forward, almost in spite of herself, then suddenly she was in my arms again, her face pressed against my shoulder. I held her lightly, not wanting to scare her off. She buried her face in my shoulder, so she wouldn't have to look me in the eye. "Oh, John . . . You killed to protect me. I know that. I know it was necessary. But . . . you don't have to be like this. So . . . cold. I could warm you." She finally looked up at me. Our eyes met, and she didn't flinch. She put her face up, and I kissed her. Because I wanted to. After a while, she stepped back, and I quickly let her go. She managed a small smile.

"Let me take you away from all this, John. Living in an insane world is bound to make you crazy. And living with a crazy woman . . ."

"She's not crazy," I said. "Just troubled."

"Of course, John."

"Suzie and I need each other."

"No you don't! Sweetie, you really don't. You need a normal, healthy relationship. I could make you happy, John, in all the ways that matter."

"How can I trust you?" I said. "You're a lust demon's daughter."

"Well," said Bettie, "no-one's perfect."

We both laughed. Sometimes . . . it's the little moments, the shared moments, that matter the most.

Alex came back, scowling as he looked from me to Bettie, and back again. "Suzie isn't answering her phone. But I've put the word out. Someone will bump into her. What do we do now?"

"I think it's way past time we sat down and watched this bloody DVD and see what's on it," I said. "You've got a player upstairs, haven't you, Alex?"

"Well, yes, but like I said I've got my new girl-friend up there . . ."

"If you think it's going to be too much for her, send her home," I said. "I'm not going one step further with this case without knowing exactly what it is I'm risking life and limb for."

"Do you really think we should?" said Bettie. " I mean, look what watching it did to poor Pen."

We all looked at Pen Donavon, back on his stool again, drinking brandy like mother's milk. He felt our gaze on him and looked round. He sighed and handed me an un-labelled DVD in a jewel case.

"Watch it, if you must," he said. "I think . . . it's sup-posed to be seen. But I couldn't bear to see it again."

"You don't have to," I said. "Stay here. The Coltranes will look after you."

But even as Alex and Bettie and I headed for the back stairs that led up to Alex's private apartment, I had to wonder what seeing the Afterlife Recording would do to us. And whether I really wanted to know the truth.

# EIGHT

*One Man's Hell*

Getting into Alex Morrisey's private apartment is never easy. He guards his privacy like a dragon with his hoard, and there are many pitfalls waiting for the unwary. I think a very specialised burglar got in once; and something ate him. First, you have to go up a set of back stairs that aren't even there unless Alex wants them to be. Then you have to pass through a series of major league protections and defences, not unlike air-locks; you can feel them opening ahead of you, then closing behind you. Any one of these traps-in-waiting would quite cheerfully kill you if given the chance, in swift, nasty, and often downright appalling ways, if Alex happened to change his mind about you at any point. I have known gang lords' crime dens that were easier to get into; and they often have their own pet demons under contract. I wouldn't even try getting into Alex's apartment without his permission unless I was armed with a tactical nuke wrapped in rabbit's feet.

But it wasn't until Alex let us into his apartment that I was really shocked. The living-room was so clean and tidy I barely recognised it. All his old junk was gone, including the charity shop furniture and his collection of frankly disturbing porcelain statuettes in pornographic poses. Replaced by comfortable furnishings and pleasant decorative touches. His books, CDs, and DVDs no longer lay scattered across all available surfaces or stacked in tottering piles against the walls; now they were all set out neatly on brand-new designer shelving. Probably in alphabetical order, too. It was actually possible now to walk across Alex's living-room without having to kick things out of the way, and his carpet didn't crunch when you trod on it.

In the end, it was the cushions on the sofa that gave it away. Men who live on their own don't have cushions. They just don't. It's a guy thing.

I looked accusingly at Alex. "You've let a woman move in with you, haven't you? Don't you ever learn?"

"I didn't say anything," Alex said haughtily, "because I knew you wouldn't approve. Besides, you're in no position to throw stones. You live with a psychopathic gun nut."

There was a noise from the next room. A small tic appeared briefly in Alex's face. I looked at him sternly. "What was that?"

"Just the vulture," Alex said quickly. "Morning sickness."

A sudden horrible thought struck me. "You haven't let your ex-wife move back in, have you?"

"I would rather projectile vomit my own intestines," said Alex, with great dignity.

"Sorry," I said.

"I should think so, too."

"Wait a minute. Downstairs in the bar, you said your new girl-friend was up here. So where is she? Why is she hiding from me? And why do I just know that I'm really not going to like the answers to any of these questions?"

"Oh, hell," said Alex. He looked back at the other room. "You'd better come in, Cathy."

And while I was standing there, struck dumb with shock, my teenage secretary, Cathy, came in from the next room. She smiled at me brightly, but I was still too stunned to respond. She was wearing a smart and sophisticated little outfit, and surprisingly understated make-up. I barely recognised her. Normally she favoured colours so fashionable they made your eye-balls bleed.

"*This* is your new girl-friend?" I said finally. "Cathy? My Cathy? My *teenage* secretary? She's almost half your age!"

"*I know!*" said Alex. "She took one look at my music collection and turned up her nose! Called it dad rock . . . But; she came into the bar one night with a message from you, and, well, we happened to get talking, and . . . we clicked. Next thing I know we're a couple, and she's moved in with me. Neither of us said anything to you because we knew you'd blow your stack."

"I am lost for words," I said.

"Bet that doesn't last," said Cathy.

I glared at her. "I did not rescue you from a house that tried to eat you, take you in, and make you my secretary, just so you could get involved with a disreputable character like Alex Morrisey!"

"I thought Alex was your friend?" said Bettie, who I felt was enjoying the situation entirely too much.

"He is. Mostly. It's because I know him so well that I'm worried! Alex has even worse luck with women than I do."

"I resent that!" said Alex.

"I notice you're not denying it," I said.

Cathy stood close beside Alex, holding his arm protectively. It reminded me of the way Bettie had been holding my arm recently. Cathy looked me square in the eye, her jaw set in a familiar and very determined manner.

"I am eighteen now, going on nineteen. I'm not the frightened little girl you rescued any more. Hell, I've been running your office for the last few years and kept all the paper-work in order, which is more than you ever did. I am old enough to run my own life and to be responsible for my own actions. Just like you always taught me. Go after what really matters to you, you said. And I did. Alex and I might not be the most . . . orthodox of couples; but then, neither are you and Suzie."

I smiled briefly. "Well. My little girl is all grown-up. All right, Cathy. You're clearly off your head and displaying quite appalling taste, but you have the right to make your own mistakes." I looked at Alex. "We will talk about this later."

"Oh, joy," said Alex.

"Quite," I said. "Now, show me how that fiendishly complicated-looking remote control works."

Alex picked up something big enough to land the space shuttle from a distance, turned on his television, dimmed the lights, and showed me how to work the DVD player.

"That button is for the surround sound, the toggle is for the volume. Don't touch that one; it turns on the sprinkler system. And stay away from that one because it operates the vibrating bed. Don't look at me like that."

"What's this big red button for?" said Bettie, sitting beside me on the sofa before the television.

"*Do not touch the big red button,*" said Alex. "That is only to be used in the event of alien invasion, or if someone not a million miles from here starts another bloody angel war."

"I did not . . ."

"Right," said Alex. "That's it. You two enjoy the show, Cathy and I will be down in the bar."

"Don't you want to see what's on the DVD?" said Bettie.

"I would rather stab myself in the eyes with knives," said Alex. "Come along, Cathy."

"But I want to watch it!" said Cathy.

"No, you don't," Alex said firmly. "Wait until John's test-driven it; then, if it's safe, we can have a peep at it."

"So I'm your guinea-pig now?" I said, amused despite myself.

"Hey," said Alex. "What are friends for?"

"If you do get Raptured," said Cathy, "can I have your trench coat?"

Alex hustled her out, leaving Bettie and me alone with the television and the Afterlife Recording. The disc looked quite remarkably ordinary, almost innocent, as I took it out of its case. I handled it gingerly, half-afraid the thing might try to bite me, or even burst into flames once exposed to the open air; but it was only a DVD. I slipped it into the machine, hit PLAY, and Bettie and I settled back to watch.

There was no menu, no introduction. It was a recording of an unexpected transmission, with the beginning missing. It just started, and the television screen showed a view into Hell. There were buildings, or more properly structures, great looming things, like impossibly huge cancers. The walls were scarlet meat traced with purple veins, sick and decaying. Suppurating holes that might have been windows showed people trapped inside, plugged into the breathing sweating architecture, sometimes sunk deep in cancerous flesh; and all of them were screaming in agony.

The structures were packed too close together, their malign presence like a concentration camp of the soul. Through the narrow streets ran an endless stream of naked sinners, burned and bleeding, sobbing and shrieking as horned demons drove them on. The sinners who fell or lagged behind were dragged down and torn apart by the demons. Only to rise again, made whole, so they could be driven on again, forever. Bodies hung from lamp-posts, still kicking and struggling, as demons tugged their intestines from great rips in their bellies.

The sky was on fire, spreading a blood-red light across the terrible scene. Huge bat-winged shapes circled overhead. And from far off in the distance, vast and terrible, came the laughter of the Devil, savouring the horrors of Hell.

I hit the PAUSE button, leaned back on the sofa, and looked at Bettie. "It's a fake. That's not Hell."

"Are you sure?" said Bettie. And then her eyes widened, and she actually leaned back a little from me. "Do you *know*? Are the stories true, that you've really been to Hell, and returned?"

"Of course not," I said. "Only one man ever returned from the Houses of Pain, and he was the Son of God. No; you can tell that isn't the real thing from looking at the sinners. They all have the same face, see? Pen Donavon's face."

Bettie leaned in close for a better look. "You're right!

All the faces are the same! Even the demons, just exaggerated versions of Pen's features. But what does this mean, John? If this isn't a recording of the Afterlife, what is it?"

I hit the STOP button and turned off the television. "It's psychic imprinting," I said. "We discussed this, remember? What we were looking at was one man's personal vision of Hell. All of Pen Donavon's fears and nightmares appeared on his television set, leaking out of his subconscious, and when he tried to record what he saw, he psychically imprinted his own vision onto the DVD. Poor bastard. He believes he belongs in Hell; though probably only he could tell us why."

"So there never was any transmission from Beyond?" said Bettie.

"No. All that junk Donavon bolted onto his television set was just junk, after all."

I removed the DVD from the player and slipped it back into its case. Such a small thing, to have caused so much trouble.

"It doesn't matter," Bettie said cheerfully. "It looks good enough to pass. Fake or no, the paper can still make decent money off it. Actually, it's even better that it's not the real thing; now we don't have to worry about upsetting anyone *Upstairs*. It looks impressive enough, and that's all the punters will care about. So what do we do now, John? Take the DVD back to the *Unnatural Inquirer* offices, along with poor Pen? We can keep him safe there, until the DVD's appeared, then we can leak the news that it's not the real thing after all, and everyone will leave him alone."

"It's not going to be that simple," I said reluctantly. "That might have worked, right up to the point where I killed all Kid Cthulhu's combat sorcerers over it. No-one will believe I'd go to so much trouble unless there was some truth to the story."

"Ah," said Bettie. "Then, what are we going to do?"

"Good question," I said. "I'm not entirely sure. We need to play this exactly right . . ."

I thought for a while, pacing up and down, rejecting one idea after another, while Bettie watched, fascinated. And finally, I got it. A very crafty and downright sneaky way out of this mess. I took out my mobile phone and called Kid Cthulhu, on his very private number.

"Hi, Kid," I said cheerfully. "This is John Taylor. How are the barnacles?"

"How did you get this number?" said Kid Cthulhu. As always, he sounded like someone drowning in his own vomit.

"I find things, remember? I know everyone's private number. Or at least, everyone who matters. You should be flattered you made the list. Now, I don't want a war with you. I've got the DVD of the Afterlife Recording right here in my hand, and I'm willing to sell it to you for a merely extortionate price."

"You killed all my combat sorcerers, didn't you?"

"Try not to dwell on the negative aspects, Kid; we can

still do business. How about I come over to your place, and we discuss it?"

"You're not coming anywhere near my place," said Kid Cthulhu. "I've just had it redecorated. How about The Witch's Tit? Down on Beltane Street? Lap dancers and the like. Very classy."

"Sounds it," I said. "Okay, meet you there in an hour."

"Why the rush?"

"Because the Removal Man is on my trail, and I want to be rid of the damned DVD before he catches up with me. You know he's already taken out the Cardinal over this? Once the DVD is yours, he'll be your problem."

"One hour," said Kid Cthulhu. "And don't bring Shotgun Suzie with you or the deal's off."

"Such a fuss, over one little tentacle," I said. "If she'd wanted you dead, you'd be dead."

"Have you seen what's on the DVD?" said Kid Cthulhu.

"Of course not," I said. "And yes; I guarantee there are no other copies. You're buying exclusive rights to the Afterlife Recording."

"One hour," said Kid Cthulhu.

The line went dead. I put the phone away, smiling. These gang bosses all think they're so smart.

"Right," I said to Bettie. "Let's go meet Captain Sushi."

"It's bound to be a trap," said Bettie. She'd had her head right next to mine, so she could listen in on the call.

"Of course it's a trap," I said. "Kid Cthulhu owns The

Witch's Tit. But since we know it's a trap going in, we can be ready to take advantage of it. What matters is setting things up so everyone will believe Kid Cthulhu has the Afterlife Recording."

"Wait a minute," said Bettie. "You can't just give it to him, John. My paper . . ."

"Relax," I said. "At exactly the right moment, you will distract him, and I will swap this DVD for one I will happen to have hidden about my person. Something from Alex's collection; he won't even know it's gone till it's too late. Kid Cthulhu will be bound to make a fuss about getting the DVD from me, and the news will be all over the Nightside by the time he actually works up the nerve to watch what he's bought. By which time we will have delivered the real thing to your paper's offices, where it will be safe. Until you give it away with this Sunday's edition. And Kid Cthulhu . . . will learn the cost of messing with me and mine."

"He'll kill you," said Bettie.

"He can join the queue."

I took an unlabelled disc from Alex's private collection of elf porn, slipped it into an inside pocket, and smiled again. The day I couldn't work a simple bait and switch like this, I'd retire.

There's a lot more to being a private eye than most people realise.

* * *

We went back down into the bar. I didn't need Alex's help to leave his apartment though I could still feel his defences, like so many spider's webs, trailing lightly against my face as I went down the stairs. Pen Donavon was still sitting slumped on his bar-stool, staring into his brandy glass. Alex was behind the bar, scowling at Donavon as he opened yet another bottle of the good brandy. For a tired, scared, and totally out-of-his-mind man on the run, Donavon could really put it away. I suppose when you believe you're going to Hell anyway, little things like hangovers and liver failure don't bother you any more.

Cathy was behind the bar with Alex, poking the meat pies with a stick to see if they needed replacing yet. Lucy and Betty Coltrane were still clearing up the general mess. Everyone turned to look as Bettie and I appeared from the back stairs.

"Well?" said Alex. "How was it? What was it? I've got a first-rate exorcist on speed dial, if you need him."

"Everyone relax," I said. "It's a fake."

Pen Donavon's head came up. "What?"

I started to explain, as kindly as I could, about psychic imprinting and guilt, but I could tell he wasn't listening. And I stopped as I realised the bar was getting darker. The light became suffused with red, as though stained with fresh blood, sinking into a deep crimson glow. Tables and chairs suddenly exploded into flames and burned fiercely, unconsumed. The Coltranes backed quickly away, and joined the rest of us at the bar. The walls slumped slowly inwards, swollen and inflamed, their fleshy texture studded with sweating tumours. A huge eye opened in the ceiling, staring down at us in cold judgement. The floor became soft and uncertain beneath my feet, heaving like the slow swell of the sea. Deep dark shadows were forming all around us, slowly closing in.

"It's him, isn't it?" said Bettie, gripping my arm with both hands. "It's Pen. He's imprinting his vision of Hell right here, with us."

"Looks like it," I said. "Only this doesn't look or feel like any illusion. I wouldn't go so far as to say it's real, as such, but it could be real enough to kill us."

"How is he doing this?" said Alex. "This bar has defences and protections laid down by Merlin himself!"

"Yes," I said. "Where is the power coming from to let him do something like this?"

I fired up my gift, and looked at Pen Donavon through my third eye, my private eye. And I found the hidden source of his unnatural power. I could See the thing, inside his body, tucked away under the sternum and over the heart. It must have come to his little shop as just another piece of interdimensional flotsam and jetsam; and he probably hadn't realised how powerful it was until he accidentally activated it. Probably hadn't even realised it was alive until it forced its way inside him. Now it was attached to him, a part of him, with long tendrils reaching into his heart and gut and brain. A mystical parasite, living off him while feeding him power in return.

I couldn't tear it out of him without killing him in the process. And I didn't want to kill Pen Donavon, even after all the trouble he'd caused. None of this was really his fault. I doubt he'd had a free and uninfluenced thought of his own since the parasite took up residence inside him.

Demons emerged from the shadows around us. Hunched and horned, with scarlet skin; medieval devils all with distorted versions of Donavon's face. They smiled to show their jagged teeth and flexed their clawed hands hungrily. Alex had his cricket bat out again. Cathy had the shotgun. Betty and Lucy Coltrane stood back-to-back, ready to take on all comers. Bettie looked at me. I looked at Pen Donavon.

"Why Hell?" I said bluntly. "Why are you so convinced of your own damnation? What could a small and insignificant little man like you have possibly done that could be so bad that all you ever think about is Hell?"

For a long moment I thought he wasn't going to answer me. The demons were getting very close. And then he sighed deeply, staring into his glass.

"I had a dog," he said. "Called him Prince. He was a good dog. Had him for years. Then I got married. She never took to Prince. Just wasn't a dog person. We all got along well enough . . . until the marriage hit problems. We started arguing over small things and worked our way up. She said she was going to leave me. I still loved her. Begged her to stay; said I'd do anything. She said I had to prove my love for her. Get rid of the dog. I loved my dog, but she was my wife. So I said I'd give Prince up. Find him a good home somewhere else. But no, that wasn't good enough. She said I had to prove she was more important to me than the dog, by killing him.

"Have Prince put down. Or she'd leave me. My choice, she said.

"I killed my dog. Took him to the vet's, said good-bye, held his paw while the vet gave him the injection. Took my dog home. Buried him.

"And she left me anyway. Prince was my dog. He was the best dog in the world. And I killed him." He looked slowly round the bar, at the Hell he'd made. Slow tears were running down his cheeks. "I deserve this. All of it."

The fires blazed up all around us. My bare skin smarted painfully from the heat. The air was thick with the stench of blood and brimstone. The demons were almost within reach. In his need to be punished, to make atonement for his sin, Pen Donavon had brought Hell to Earth; or something close enough to do the job. He could burn up the whole bar and everyone in it . . . but the parasite inside him would make sure he survived. To go on suffering. Suddenly I knew what the parasite fed on.

I got angry then. I could kill Donavon, rip the parasite right out of him. But he didn't deserve that. Not when there was a better way. I'm John Taylor, and I find things. Things, and people, and just sometimes, a way out of Hell for those who need it.

I raised my gift and forced my inner eye all the way open, making it look in a direction I normally had sense enough to avoid. I concentrated, drawing on every resource I had, and I Saw beyond this world and into the

Next. I found who I was looking for and called his name; and he came. A great door opened up in the middle of the bar, spilling a bright and brilliant light into the crimson glare, forcing it back. All the demons stopped and looked round, as a great mongrel dog with a shaggy head and drooping ears bounded out of the door and into the bar. He went straight for the demons nearest Donavon, and tore right through them, gripping them with his powerful jaws and shaking them back and forth like a terrier with a rat. The demons cried out miserably, and fell apart. Donavon looked at the dog, and his whole face lit up in amazed disbelief.

*"Prince?"*

"Typical," said the dog, spitting out a bit of demon, then trotting over to push his great shaggy head into Donavon's lap. "Can't turn my back on you for five minutes."

"I'm so sorry, Prince. I'm so sorry." Donavon could hardly get the words out. He bent over and hugged the dog round the neck.

"It's all right," said the dog. "Humans can't think for shit when they're in heat. It was her fault, not yours. You were just weak; she was the bad one."

"Do you forgive me, Prince?"

"Of course; that's what dogs do. Another good reason why all dogs go to Heaven. Now come along with me, Pen. It's time to go."

Donavon looked at the wonderful light falling out of

the door in the middle of the bar. "But . . . you're dead, Prince."

"Yes. And so are you. You've been dead ever since that parasite ate its way into you. Don't you remember? No; I suppose it won't let you. Either way, it's only the parasite's energies that have been keeping you going, so it could feed on your pain and fear." The dog paused. "You know, there's nothing like being dead for increasing your vocabulary. I've been so much more articulate since I crossed over. Anyone got a biscuit? No? Come with me, Pen. Heaven awaits."

"Will we be together, Prince?"

"Of course, Pen. Forever and ever and ever."

There was a bright flash of light, and when it faded the bar was back to normal again. The Hell that Pen Donavon had made was gone, and so was the door full of light. His dead body slumped slowly forward and fell off the stool, hitting the floor. It heaved suddenly, jerked this way and that by loud cracking and tearing sounds, and then the parasite appeared from under the body. It scuttled across the floor like a huge beetle, until I stepped forward and stamped down hard. It crunched satisfyingly under my boot, and was still.

Gone straight to Hell, where it belonged.

# NINE

*Entrances and Exits*

So, back to Uptown we went. It had been a long time since I'd been involved with a case that involved so much walking, and I was getting pretty damned tired of it. If I'd wanted to spend so much time tramping back and forth in the Nightside, wearing out good shoe leather and guaranteeing severe lower back pain for later, I'd have had my head examined. And to add insult to injury, a fog had come up, ghosting the Nightside in shades of pearl and grey. Fog is always a bad sign; it means the barriers between the worlds are wearing thin. You can never tell what might appear out of the mists or disappear into them.

The Witch's Tit aspired to dreams of class and opulence,

but it was really just another titty bar with a theme. A campy mixture of Goth come-ons and Halloween kitsch, where the girls danced naked, apart from tall witch's hats, and did obscene things with their broomsticks. The club was situated right on the very edge of Uptown, as though the other establishments were ashamed of it, and quite probably they were. The Witch's Tit was the only legitimate business Kid Cthulhu owned and certainly the only one he took a personal interest in.

Why? Well, here's a hint: word has it he's not a leg man.

The club itself looked cheap and tacky from the outside, all sleazy neon and seedy photos of girls who probably didn't even work there, but that wasn't what concerned me. There was no barker outside, singing the praises of the girls and cajoling passers-by to come on in and take a look. And when I cautiously pushed the door open and looked inside, there weren't any bouncers either, or any traces of security. Kid Cthulhu wasn't known for leaving his assets undefended, especially during an important meet like this. Had to be a trap of some kind. So I walked in, smiling cheerfully, with Bettie bouncing happily along at my side in a black leather outfit with chains and studs, and a perky little dog collar round her throat.

The club had been fitted out with all the usual Halloween motifs—black walls, witch's cauldrons, and grinning pumpkin-heads. The lighting was comfortably dim and inviting, save for half a dozen spotlights that stabbed down onto the raised stage at the back of the club, picking out the dancer's steel poles. But still; no girls, no customers, no bar staff. Kid Cthulhu had cleared the place out, just for me. The phrase *no witnesses* was whispering in the back of my head. I led Bettie through the empty tables and out into the open space before the stage, our footsteps loud and carrying in the quiet. Half a dozen human skeletons had been hung from stretchy elastic, bobbing gently at the edge of the open space, perhaps disturbed by our approach. At first I thought they were another example of the Halloween décor, but something made me stop and take a closer look. They were all real skeletons, the bones held together by copper wire. Some of the longer bones showed teeth-marks.

A new spotlight stabbed down from overhead, revealing Kid Cthulhu sitting on a huge reinforced chair, right in the centre of the open space. He looked like a man, but he wasn't. Not any more. You could tell. You could see it, feel it. There was a taint in the man, all the way through. He had been touched, and changed, by something from Outside. Kid Cthulhu was a large man, he had to be, to contain everything that was in him now. He was naked, his skin stretched taut and swollen, as though pushed out by pressures from within. He was supposed to be about my age, but his face was so puffed out no trace of human character remained in it. He sat slumped in his oversized chair, like King Glutton on his throne. His bare skin gleamed dully in the mercilessly revealing spotlight, colourless as a fish's belly, while his eyes were all black, like a shark's.

They say he broke men's bones with his bare hands. They say he ate the flesh of men, breaking open the bones to get at the marrow. They said there was something growing within him, or perhaps through him, from Outside. And right then, I believed every word they said.

"Hey, KC," I said cheerfully. "Where's the Sunshine Band?"

He studied me coldly with his flat black eyes. "John Taylor . . . Your name is bile and ashes in my mouth. Your presence here is an affront to me. Your continued existence an unbearable insult. You killed my combat sorcerers. My boys. My lovely boys."

"You have changed," I said. "You never should have gone on that deep-sea voyage. Or at the very least, you should have thrown back what you caught."

"You defy me," said Kid Cthulhu. "No-one does that any more. I shall enjoy killing you."

His voice was harsh and laboured, forced out word by word, with a distinct gurgle in it, as though he were speaking underwater. He sounding like a drowning man, venting his spite on the man who'd pushed him in.

"I thought we were here to do business," I said. "I have the Afterlife Recording right here with me."

"I don't care about that any more," said Kid Cthulhu. "Money doesn't matter to me. I have money. All that matters now is the satisfying of my various appetites and the destruction of my enemies. I will see you broken, suffering, and dead, John Taylor. And your pretty little companion. Perhaps I'll make you watch as I tear her guts out, and eat them as she dies, screaming."

"Oh, ick," said Bettie. "Nasty man . . ."

Kid Cthulhu rose suddenly up from his throne, a man twice the size a man should be, forcing his great bulk up onto its feet through sheer strength of will. His joints were buried deep under swollen flesh, and unnaturally distended genitals showed under the great swell of his belly.

"Double ick," said Bettie. "With a side order of not even for a million pounds."

Kid Cthulhu strode toward us, slowly and deliberately, each step shaking the floor, his deep-set eyes fixed on me. His purple pouting mouth parted to reveal jagged sharp teeth. His huge puffy hands opened to reveal claws. Someone that size shouldn't have been able to move unaided, let alone have such an air of strength and deadly purpose. I was still thinking what to do when Bettie stepped smartly forward, opened her purse, took out her Mace spray, and let Kid Cthulhu have it, right in the face.

"Nasty fat man," she said calmly. "And you smell."

Kid Cthulhu stopped before her, surprised, but showing no hurt at all from a faceful of Mace laced with holy water. His all-black eyes barely blinked as the Mace ran down his distended cheeks like so many viscous tears. He lashed out suddenly, one huge arm swinging round impossibly quickly, and the impact knocked Bettie off her feet and sent her flying. She crashed through a table, hit the floor hard, rolled over a few times, and lay still; and it was all over before I could even move a muscle. I called out to her, but she didn't answer. And then Kid Cthulhu turned his head and looked at me.

He was between me and Bettie, so I couldn't get to her. I backed away slowly, thinking fast. I hadn't planned for this. I'd heard he was going through changes, but I still thought of him as just another gang boss. Someone I could make a deal with. The Nightside runs on deals. But all this Kid Cthulhu wanted was me, preferably in large meaty chunks. I don't normally care to get involved with hand-to-hand combat, partly because it's coarse and vulgar and beneath my dignity, but mostly because I've never been that good at it. I've always preferred to talk or threaten or bluff my way out of trouble. But I didn't think that was going to work here.

I stopped, stood my ground, and stared him right in the eye. Sometimes the oldest tricks are the best. But for the second time that day, I found myself faced with someone I couldn't stare down. His flat black eyes stared right back at me, untouched and unmoved. I couldn't reach him. I wasn't even sure there was anything human left in him to reach. So I grabbed the nearest chair and threw it at him. It bounced off, without leaving a single mark on his veiny, distended skin.

Then he was coming right at me, a huge mass of colourless flesh like something you'd find at the bottom of the sea, driven on by some unnatural energy. I'd beaten so many threats in my time, faced down and defeated so many Major Players, gods, and monsters . . . It had never occurred to me that I might be killed by some oversized, implacable gang boss.

As he crashed forward, the floor shaking with every tread, I somehow found the time to notice that his flesh seemed to move more slowly than the rest of him, sliding across his deep-sunk bones like an afterthought, as though it wasn't properly connected any more. What little humanity he had left in him was sliding away. I glanced behind me. I could have run. I was pretty sure I could beat him to the exit. But that would have meant leaving Bettie behind, abandoned to Kid Cthulhu's inhuman appetites. He'd said he'd do terrible things to her, and I believed him. So I stepped forward, braced myself, and punched him right in his protruding belly. His impetus drove him forward onto my fist, and it sank deep into his gut. He didn't even make a sound. The cold, cold flesh closed around my hand, sucking it in. I had to use all my strength to pull it free again. Just the touch of his flesh was enough to set my teeth on edge.

A huge arm came swinging round out of nowhere and hit me like a club. I managed to get a shoulder round in time to take the worst of the impact, but the flesh seemed to just keep coming and slammed into the side of my face. The strength went out of my legs, and I hit the floor hard, driving the breath from my lungs. My left shoulder blazed with pain, and I could barely move my left arm. The whole left side of my face ached fiercely. There was blood in my mouth, and I spat it out. I sensed as much as saw Kid Cthulhu looming over me, and I rolled to one side as his great fist came slamming down like a pile-driver, cracking and splintering the floor where I'd been lying. I got my legs under me and forced myself back up onto my feet again. I didn't feel too steady, and I was breathing hard. Kid Cthulhu wasn't.

I backed away. My left eye was puffing shut, and it felt like my nose might be broken. I checked my teeth with my tongue. I didn't seem to have lost any, this time. I hate it when that happens. There was more blood in my mouth. Probably a cut on the inside of my cheek. I spat the blood in Kid Cthulhu's direction, but his flat dark eyes never wavered.

I couldn't fight a man like this. I had to be smarter than that.

I backed away some more, glancing round to make sure I was leading Kid Cthulhu away from Bettie, and then made myself concentrate past the pain. I called up my gift, and looked at Kid Cthulhu with my inner eye. If I couldn't fight the man, maybe I could fight what was inside him. I used my gift to find the taint, the inhuman corruption deep within his flesh, the thing from Outside that was slowly suffusing his human form. And having found it, it was the easiest thing in the world to rip the taint right out of him.

Kid Cthulhu screamed; and for the first time, he sounded human. He fell to his knees, no longer able to sustain his massive weight once the taint from Outside was gone. He fell forward onto his face, his flesh moving in great ripples of fat. And beside him stood the taint, a horrid twisting shape that made no sense at all in only three spatial dimensions. It howled its fury, in a voice I heard more with my mind than my ears. It didn't belong in this world, stripped of the host it had been transforming into something suitable to birth its new form. I wondered briefly what that might have been. Nothing like Kid Cthulhu, certainly. It hurt just to look at the taint. Like a colour too vile for our spectrum, a shape like a living Rorschach blot that suggested only nightmares. Its very presence in this world was like fingernails scraping down the blackboard of my soul.

It came after me, moving in ways unknown in my comfortable, three-dimensional world. I ran for the raised stage at the back of the club, and it followed. It moved more like energy than anything physical, and that gave me an idea. Up on the stage, I backed slowly away. A bolt of vivid energy snapped out, and I had to throw myself to one side to avoid it. The taint came after me, rising and falling in the air. My back slammed up against a steel dancer's pole. The taint fired another energy bolt. I ducked to one side, and the energy bolt hit the steel pole. The taint screamed as its energy grounded through the pole, discharging into the earth below, its howl rising and rising till it seemed to fill my head, and then the sound broke off as the taint disappeared, gone.

Now that I was out of danger, my arm and my shoulder and my face all hurt worse than ever, but I made myself get down from the stage and go over to where Bettie was still lying sprawled on the floor. As I approached, she raised her head a little, looked at me, then sat up easily.

"Is it over?" she said brightly. "I thought I'd better keep my head down, and not get in your way." And then she saw the state of my face and scrambled to her feet. "Oh, John, sweetie, you're hurt! What did he do to you?"

She produced a clean white handkerchief from somewhere, licked it briefly with a pointed tongue, and dabbed cautiously at my face, wiping the blood away. It hurt, but I let her do it. My left eye was puffed shut, but at least I'd stopped spitting blood.

"Looks worse than it is," I said, trying to convince myself as much as Bettie.

"Hush," she said. "Stand still. My hero."

When she'd finished, she looked at the bloody handkerchief, pulled a face, and tucked it up one black leather sleeve. I looked thoughtfully at Kid Cthulhu, still lying where he'd fallen like a beached whale. I walked slowly over to him, Bettie trotting at my side. She managed to make it clear she was there to be leaned on, if necessary, but was considerate enough not to say it out loud. I stood over Kid Cthulhu, and he rolled his flat black eyes up in his stretched face to look at me.

"Kill you, Taylor. Kill you for this. Kill you, and all your friends, and everyone you know. I have people. I'll send them after you, and I'll never stop, never. Never!"

"I believe you," I said. And I raised my foot and stamped down hard, right on the back of his fat neck. I felt as much as heard his neck break under my foot, and as easily as that the life went out of him. I stepped back. Bettie looked at me, horrified.

"You killed him. Just like that. How could you?"

"Because it was necessary," I said "You heard him."

"But . . . I never thought of you as a cold-blooded killer . . . You're supposed to be better than that!"

"Mostly I am," I said. "But no-one threatens me and mine."

"I don't know you at all, do I?" Bettie said slowly, looking at me steadily.

"I'm just . . . who I have to be," I said.

And then we both looked round sharply. Someone new was there in the club with us, though I hadn't heard him come in. He was standing on the raised stage, in a spotlight of his own, waiting patiently to be noticed. A tall and slender man with dark coffee-coloured skin, wearing a smartly cut pale grey suit, with an apricot cravat at his throat. He might have been any age, but there was an air of experience and quiet authority about him. As though he had so much power he didn't need to put on a show. His head was shaven, gleaming in the spotlight. His eyes were kind, his smile pleasant; and I didn't trust him an inch.

"You did well, in dealing with Kid Cthulhu," he said finally, in a rich, smooth and cultured voice. "A very unpleasant fellow, destined to become something even more unpleasant. I would have taken care of him myself, in time, but you did a good job, Mr. Taylor."

"And you are?" I said. "Though I have a horrible suspicion I already know."

"I am the Removal Man. An honourable calling, in a dishonourable world. And I am here for the Afterlife Recording."

"Of course you are," I said. "It's been that sort of a day. How did you know I was bringing it here?"

"Mr. Taylor," the Removal Man said reproachfully, "I know what I need to know. It's part of my function. Now be a good chap and hand over the DVD, and we can get through this without any . . . unpleasantness. It must be removed; it's far too great a temptation for all concerned."

"The *Unnatural Inquirer* owns exclusive rights to the Afterlife Recording," said Bettie automatically, though I could tell she was getting tired of having to tell people that.

"I do not recognise the Law, or its bindings," the Removal Man said easily. "I answer to a higher calling. Just hand over the DVD, Mr. Taylor, and I'll be on my way. This doesn't have to end badly. You must admit that the Nightside will be better off without the Recording. Look how much trouble it's already caused."

"You don't need to do anything," I said. I was trying very hard to sound casual and reasonable, like him. It's not easy talking to someone who can probably make you disappear off the face of the Earth just by thinking about it. I added the *probably* as a sop to my pride, but I really didn't want to get into a pissing contest with the Removal Man. I had the uneasy feeling that his legend might be a little bit more real than mine. "I've seen what's on the DVD, and it's nothing you need be concerned about. It's a fake, the psychic imprinting of a disturbed mind."

"You've seen it?" said the Removal Man, raising one elegant eyebrow. "Oh, dear. How very unfortunate. Now I have to take care of you as well."

"But . . . I've seen it, too!" said Bettie. "It's nothing! It's a fake!"

The Removal Man shook his shaven head sadly, still smiling his kind smile. "Yes, well, you would say that, wouldn't you?"

"You can't just make us disappear!" Bettie said defiantly. "I work for the *Unnatural Inquirer*! I have the full resources of the paper behind me. And this is John Taylor! You know who his friends are. You really want Razor Eddie or Dead Boy coming after you? And anyway, what makes you so sure you're always right? What makes you infallible? What gives you the right to judge the whole world and everyone in it?"

"Ah," he said, smugly. "The secret origin of the Removal Man; is that what you want, little miss demon girl reporter? Yes, I know who you are, Miss Divine. I know who everyone is. Very well, then; I sold my soul to God. In return for power over the Earth and everything in it. Not God himself, as such, one of his representatives. But the deal is just as real. I am here to pass judgement on the wicked; and I do. Because someone has to. I'm changing the Nightside for the better; one thing, one person, one soul at a time. You mustn't worry, Miss Divine. It won't hurt a bit. Though really, gentlemen should go first. Isn't that right, Mr. Taylor?"

Bettie moved immediately to put herself between me and the Removal Man. "You can't! I won't let you! He's a good man, in his way. And he's done more for the Nightside than you ever have!"

"Stand aside," said the Removal Man. "Mr. Taylor goes first, because he is the most dangerous. And please, no more protestations. I really have heard them all before."

Bettie was still searching for something to say, when I took her by the arm and moved her gently but firmly to one side. "I don't hide behind anyone," I said to the Removal Man. "I don't need to, you arrogant, self-righteous little prig."

"Mr. Taylor . . ."

"What did you have to kill the Cardinal for? I liked him. He was no threat to anyone."

"He betrayed his faith," said the Removal Man. "He was a thief. And an abomination."

"I've scraped more appealing things than you off the bottom of my shoe," I said.

I raised my gift again and Saw right through the Removal Man. It wasn't difficult to find out who he'd really made his deal with and show him the truth. Not God. Not God at all. I showed the Removal Man who'd really been pulling his strings all this time, and he screamed like a soul newly damned to Hell. He staggered back and forth on the raised stage, shaking his head in denial, even as he cried out in shock and loathing. Until finally, unable to face who and what he really was, he turned his power on himself and disappeared.

And that was the end of the Removal Man.

I hadn't wanted to destroy him. He really had done a lot of good in his time, along with the bad and the questionable. But no-one's more vulnerable than those who believe they're better than everyone else. His whole existence had been based on a lie. He'd been betrayed, and I knew who by. I'd Seen him. I looked into the shadows at the back of the raised stage.

"All right, you can come out now. Come on out, Mr. Gaylord du Rois, Editor of the one and only *Unnatural Inquirer*."

Bettie's gasp was so shocked it came out as little more than a muffled squeak as Gaylord du Rois stepped forward into the light to stare calmly down at both of us.

"Well done, Mr. Taylor. You really are almost as good as people say you are."

Du Rois was a tall, elderly gentleman, dressed in the very best Edwardian finery. His back was straight, his head held high, and there wasn't a trace of weakness or frailty in him, for all his obvious age. His face was a mass of wrinkles, and his bare head was undecorated save for liver spots and a few fly-away hairs. His deep-set cold grey eyes hardly blinked at all, and his mouth was a wet slash of colourless lips. His hands were withered claws, but they still looked like they could do a lot of damage. He burned with a harsh and unforgiving energy, determined and defiant, as though he could hold back death through sheer force of will. He nodded at the spot where the Removal Man had disappeared himself.

"Damned fool. Always was inflexible. He really did think he'd been given his power by God himself, to indulge his prejudices and paranoias. I suppose learning I was his puppet master, and had been all along, was just too much to bear. Such a come-down from God. It doesn't matter. I'd have had to replace him soon anyway. He was having delusions of independence. Still, I can always find another fool."

"I don't understand," said Bettie. "You're the Editor? You've always been the Editor? And . . . the Removal Man was your creature all along? Why?"

"Dear Bettie," du Rois said indulgently. "Always a reporter, always asking the right questions. Yes, my dear, I am your Editor and always have been. The *Inquirer* is mine, and mine alone, and has been for over a hundred years. And in that time I have created many Removal Men to serve my needs. They don't tend to last long. Such small, blinkered, black-and-white attitudes don't tend to survive long when faced with the ever-shifting greys of the Nightside. They burn out. But there's always someone who thinks they know better than everyone else, just itching for a chance to remake the world in their own limited image . . ."

"Why create them?" I said. "I don't see why the Editor of the *Unnatural Inquirer* should give much of a damn about the morality of the Nightside."

"Quite right, Mr. Taylor. I don't give a damn. Except for when it makes good copy. Reporting and condemning the sins and shames of the Nightside has filled the pages of my paper for generations. But one lifetime wasn't enough for me. I wanted more. There was still so much left to see, and know, and do. So I found a way. You can always find a way in the Nightside, even if some of them aren't very nice. When one of my Removal Men removes a thing, or a person, all their potential energy, from all the things they might have done, is left up for grabs; and it all comes to me. Those energies have kept me going long after I should have left this world, and made me very powerful indeed."

"You're the one who shut down my gift!" I said.

"Yes," du Rois said calmly. "It was necessary to neuter you, so you wouldn't find Pen Donavon too quickly. I needed time for rumours about the Afterlife Recording to spread, and grow, and fascinate the minds of my readers. Bringing you in guaranteed that people would pay attention. After all, if you were involved, it must be important. By the time my Sunday edition comes out, with my give-away DVD, people will be fighting for copies of my paper. And all because of you . . ."

"Sales?" I said. "This has all been about sales?"

"Of course. I don't think you appreciate exactly how much money I stand to make out of this, Mr. Taylor."

"Why are you here?" Bettie said suddenly. "Why reveal the truth about yourself now, to us?"

Du Rois smiled on her almost fondly. "Still asking the

right questions, Bettie, like the fine reporter you are. A pity you'll never get to write this story. Sorry, my dear, but I am here to protect my interests, and my paper's. And your story, of the truth behind the Afterlife Recording, can never be allowed to see print. I report the news; I have no wish to be part of it."

"You want the DVD?" I said. I took it out of my coat-pocket and threw it at him. "Have it. Damn thing's just a fake anyway."

He made no attempt to catch the disc, letting it fall to clatter on the stage before him. "Real or fake, it doesn't matter. I can still sell it, thanks to your involvement. You really have been very helpful to me, Mr. Taylor, spreading the story and stirring up interest, but that's all over now. I have my story. And since every story needs a good end-ing . . . what better way to convince everyone of the DVD's importance than that you should be killed, acquir-ing it for me? Nothing like a famous corpse to add spice to a story." He looked at Bettie. "I'm afraid you have to die, too, my dear. Can't have anyone hanging around to contradict the story I'm going to sell people."

"But . . . I'm one of your people!" said Bettie. "I work for the *Inquirer*!"

"I have lots of reporters. I can always get more. Now hush, dear. Your voice really is very wearing . . . Don't move, Mr. Taylor. I've already taken the precaution of shutting down your gift again, just in case you were thinking of using it on me. And you don't have anything else powerful enough to stop me."

"Want to bet?" I said. And I took out of my coat-pocket the Aquarius Key. I activated the small metal box, and it opened up, unfolding and blossoming like a steel flower. A great rip appeared in reality, right in front of Gaylord du Rois. He only had time to scream once before the void swallowed him, then he was gone. I hung on grimly to Bettie as the void pulled us forward, then I shut the Aquarius Key down again, and that was that.

It was suddenly very quiet in the empty club. Bettie looked at me with huge eyes.

"I really should have handed the Key over to Walker, after that nasty business at Fun Faire," I said. "But I had a feeling it might come in handy."

"You've had that all along?" said Bettie. "Why didn't you use it before?"

I shrugged. "I didn't need it before."

She hit me.

# EPILOGUE

I phoned Walker and arranged to meet him at the Londinium Club. Now that I'd used the Aquarius Key, Walker was bound to know I had it. And he'd want it. I could have hung on to the Key if I'd been ready to make a big thing out of it, but I wasn't. The Aquarius Key gave me the creeps. Some things you know are bad news for all concerned. They're just too . . . tempting. So back to the Londinium Club Bettie and I went. Plenty of time yet to take the damned DVD to the offices of the *Unnatural Inquirer*. Where Scoop Malloy would have to decide what to do with it, and the news that his paper no longer had an Editor.

"But how would Walker know you've got the Key?" said Bettie, skipping merrily along beside me. She was back in her polka-dot dress and big floppy hat look.

"Walker knows everything," I said. "Or at least, everything he needs to know."

"I still can't get over my Editor being the Bad Guy in all this. I wonder who'll replace him at the *Inquirer*?"

"Scoop Malloy?"

"Oh, please! I don't think so!" Bettie pulled a disparaging face that still somehow managed to look attractive on her. "Scoop's only Sub-Editor material, and he knows it. No; the new owner will have to bring in someone new, from outside. But you know what? I don't care! Because for the first time in my career I have a *real* story to write! The truth behind Gaylord du Rois, the Removal Men, and the Afterlife Recording. Real news . . . which means I'm a real reporter at last! Right?"

"I don't see why not," I said. "The *Inquirer* might make you the new Editor on the strength of it."

"Oh, poo! I'm not wasting a *real* story on the *Inquirer*!" Bettie said indignantly. "Far too good for them. No; I'm going to sell it to Julien Advent at the *Night Times*; in return for a job on his paper. A real reporter on a real newspaper! I'm going up in the world! Mummy will be so pleased . . ."

"What about your other story?" I said. "A day in the company of the infamous John Taylor?"

Bettie smiled and hooked her arm familiarly through mine. "Let someone else write it."

We came at last to the Londinium Club, and Bettie and I stopped at the foot of the steps to stare at the black iron railings surrounding the club. Impaled on the iron spikes were three recently severed heads. Queen Helena, Uptown Taffy Lewis, and General Condor. Helena looked as though she was still screaming. Taffy looked sullen. And the General . . . had a look of sad resignation, as though he'd known all along it would come to this. I'm sure enough people warned him. The Nightside does so love to break a hero.

"Admiring the display?" said Walker, unhurriedly descending the steps to join us. "It makes a statement, I think."

"Your work?" I asked.

"I ordered it done," said Walker. "They disturbed the peace of the Nightside and threatened to plunge it into civil war. So I did what I had to."

"And not at all because they challenged your authority," I said.

Walker just smiled.

"But . . . why kill the General?" said Bettie, staring fascinated at the impaled heads. "I mean, he was one of the good guys. Wasn't he?"

"There's no-one more dangerous to the status quo," I said. "Right, Walker?"

He put out a hand to me. "You have something for me, I believe?"

I handed over the Aquarius Key. Walker hefted it on the palm of his hand. "You didn't really think you'd be allowed to keep something as powerful as this, did you, John?"

I shrugged. "Be grateful. I could have given it to the Collector."

He nodded to me, tipped his bowler hat to Bettie, and went back into his Club. Leaving his handiwork behind him, *pour décourager les autres*.

"You could have kept that Key," said Bettie. "He's not powerful enough to make you do anything you don't want to."

"Maybe," I said. "Maybe not. All depends on where he's getting his power from these days . . . But anyway, I'm not ready to go head to head with him, not just yet. Certainly not over a glorified magical waste disposal. We're still on the same side. I think."

"Even after this?" said Bettie, gesturing fiercely at the severed heads. "Look at them! Killed by one of his pet assassins, just because they threatened his position! You liked the General. I could tell."

"Walker's done worse, in his time," I said. "And so have I."

Bettie took both my hands in hers and made me face her, her eyes holding mine. "You're better than you think, John. Better than you allow yourself to believe. I know you've done . . . questionable things. I've seen some of them. But you're not the cold-blooded killer your legend makes you out to be."

"Bettie . . ."

"You're the way you are because of *her*! Because of Suzie Shooter, Shotgun Suzie! She wants you to be a killer, just like her. Because that's the only way you'll ever have something in common instead of what everyone else has.

You don't have to be like her, John. I can show you a better life."

"Bettie, don't . . ."

"Hush, John. Hush. Listen to me. I love you. I want to be with you, want you to be with me. You can't throw your life away on Suzie Shooter, simply because you feel sorry for her. She's cold, broken . . . she can never be a real woman to you. Not like I can. How can you have a real relationship with someone when you can't even touch her? I could make you so happy, John. We could have a home, a life, a sex life."

She moved in close, still holding on tight to my hands, her face so close to mine now I could feel the breath from her words on my mouth.

"I can be any kind of woman you want, John. Every dream you ever had. I'm exactly the right kind of woman for you, one foot in Heaven, one foot in Hell. Come with me, John. You know you want to."

"Yes," I said. "I want to. But that's not enough."

"What else is there? I can help you! You don't have to be a killer, don't have to be so cold . . . With my help you could be a better person, a real hero!"

"But that's not me," I said. "And never was. I am what I have to be, to get things done; and that includes the bad as well as the good. Suzie understands that. She's always understood me. She accepts me, all of me. I've never had to explain myself to her. She's my friend, my partner, my love. I love her, and she loves me as best she can. And she cares about the real me, not the legend you still insist on seeing when you look at me. I want you, Bettie. But I don't need you, not the way I need Suzie."

"But . . . *why?*"

"Perhaps because . . . monsters belong together," I said.

I looked at her until she let go of my hands. She was breathing hard.

"Hello, John," said a cold, steady voice above us. "Is that girl bothering you?"

"Not any more," I said. "Hello, Suzie."

She was standing at the top of the steps leading down from the Londinium Club, a tall blonde Valkyrie in black motorcycle leathers, one hand tucked into the bandoliers of bullets criss-crossing her chest. She came unhurriedly down to join us. Bettie looked at her, and then at me, and then tossed her head angrily.

"You deserve each other! I never want to see you again, John Taylor!"

She strode away, her high heels clacking loudly on the pavement, her head held high. She didn't look back once.

"Nice horns," said Suzie. "Did I miss something?"

"Not really," I said. "You finished work now?"

"Yes. Just picked up my payment from Walker. A little private work." Suzie looked at the three severed heads. "Didn't take me long."

I looked at her, and then at the heads. I could have said something, but I didn't.

"Come on, Suzie," I said. "Let's go home."

It's the Nightside.

Turn the page for a special preview of
Simon R. Green's next novel

## JUST ANOTHER JUDGEMENT DAY

Available now in hardcover from Ace Books

## At Home with John and Suzie

Until Walker's people arrived, Suzie and I stuck around, talking to the newly awakened patients, and comforting them as best we could. Well, I did most of the talking and comforting. Suzie isn't really a people person. Mostly she stood at the door with her shotgun at the ready, to assure the patients that no-one was going to be allowed to mess with them any more. A lot of them were confused, and even more were in various states of shock. The physical injuries might have been reversed, but you can't undergo that kind of extended suffering without its leaving a mark on your soul.

Some of them knew each other, and sat together on the beds, holding each other and sobbing in quiet relief. Some were scared of everyone, including Suzie and me. Some . . . just didn't wake up.

Walker's people would know what to do. They had a lot of experience at picking up the pieces after someone's grand scheme has suddenly gone to hell in a hand-cart. They'd get the people help and see them safely back to their home dimension. Then they'd shut down the Timeslip, and slap a heavy fine on the Mammon Emporium for losing track of the damn thing in the first place. If people can't look after their Timeslips properly, they shouldn't be allowed to have them. Walker's people . . . would do all the things I couldn't do.

When Suzie and I finally left the Guaranteed New You Parlour, Percy D'Arcy was outside waiting for us. His fine clothes looked almost shabby, and his eyes were puffy from crying. He came at me as though he meant to attack me, and stopped only when Suzie drew her shotgun and trained it on him with one easy move. He glared at me piteously, wringing his hands together.

*"What have you done, Taylor? What have you done?"*

"I found out what was going on, and I put a stop to it," I said. "I saved a whole bunch of innocent people from . . ."

"I don't care about them! What do they matter? What have you done to my friends?" He couldn't speak for a moment, his eyes clenched shut to try to stop the tears streaming down his face. "I saw the most beautiful people of my generation reduced to hags and lepers! Saw their pretty faces fall and crack and split apart. Their hair fell out, and their backs bent, and they cried and shrieked and

screamed, running mad in the night. I saw them break out
in boils and pus and rot! *What did you do to them?*"

"I'm sorry," I said. "But they earned it."

"They were my friends," said Percy D'Arcy. "I've known
them since I was so high. I never meant for this to happen."

"Percy . . ." I said.

"You can whistle for your fee!" said Percy, with almost
hysterical dignity. And then he spun around and walked
away, still crying.

I let him go. I saw his point, sort of. Some cases, no-one
gets to feel good afterwards. So Suzie and I went home.

The Nightside doesn't have suburbs, as such. But a few
areas are a little more safe and secure than anywhere else,
where people can live quietly and not be bothered. Not
gated communities, because gates wouldn't even slow
down the kind of predators the Nightside attracts, but instead small communities protected by a few magical defences, a handful of force shields, and a really good mutual
defence pact. Besides, if you can't look after yourself, you
shouldn't be living in the Nightside anyway. Suzie and I
lived together in a nice little detached house (three up,
three down, two sideways) in one of the more peaceful and
up-market areas. Just by living there, we were driving the
house prices down, but we tried not to worry about that
too much. Originally, there was a small garden out front,
but since Suzie and I were in no way gardening people, the
first thing we did was dig it up and put in a mine-field.

We're not big on visitors. Actually, Suzie did most of the work, while I added some man-traps and a few invisible floating curses, to show I was taking an interest.

Our immediate neighbours are a time-travelling adventurer called Garth the Eternal, a big Nordic type who lived in a scaled-down Norman castle, complete with its own gargoyles who kept us awake at night during the mating season, and a cold-faced, black-haired alien hunter from the future named Sarah Kingdom, who lived in a conglomeration of vaguely organic shapes that apparently also functioned as her star-ship, if she could only find the right parts to repair it.

We've never even discussed having a housing association.

Suzie and I live on separate floors. She has the ground floor, I have the top floor, and we share the amenities. All very civilised. We spend as much time in each other's company as we can. It's not easy being either of us. My floor is defiantly old-fashioned, even Victorian. They understood a lot about comfort and luxury. That particular night, I was lying flat on my back in the middle of my four-poster bed. The goose-feather mattress was deep enough to sink into, with a firm support underneath. Some mornings Suzie had to pry me out of bed with a crow-bar. Supposedly Queen Elizabeth I had slept in the four-poster once, on one of her grand tours. Considering what the thing cost me, she should have done cart-wheels in it.

A carefully constructed fire crackled quietly in the huge stone grate, supplying just enough warmth to ward off the cold winds that blew outside. The wood in the fire remained eternally unconsumed, thanks to a simple moebius spell, so the fire never went out. One wall of my bedroom is taken up with bookshelves, mostly Zane Grey and Louis L'Amour Westerns, and a whole bunch of old John Creasey thrillers, of which I am inordinately fond. Another wall is mostly hidden behind a great big fuck-off wide-screen plasma television, facing the bed. And the final wall holds my DVDs and CDs, all in strict alphabetical order, which Suzie never ceases to make remarks about.

I have gas lighting in my bedroom. It gives a friendlier light, I think.

A richly detailed Persian rug covers most of the floor. It's supposed to have been a flying carpet at some point, but no-one can remember the activating Words any more, so it's just a rug. Except I always have to be very careful about what I say out loud while I'm standing on it. Scattered about the room are various and assorted odds and ends I've collected and acquired down the years, often as part or even full payment for a case. A few purported Objects of Power, some antiques with interesting histories, and a whole bunch of things that might or might not turn out to be valuable or useful someday.

There's a musical box that plays top-twenty hits from thirty years in the future. Still mostly crap . . . Some *Tyrannosaurus rex* dung, in a sealed glass jar, labelled *For when any old shit just won't do.* A brass head that could supposedly predict the future, though I've never heard it utter a word. And a single bloodred rose in a long glass vase. It doesn't need watering, and it hisses angrily if anyone gets too close, so mostly I leave it alone. It's only there to add a spot of colour.

As I lay on top of the blankets on my huge bed, listening to the wind battering outside and feeling all warm and cosy, it occurred to me how far I'd come since I returned to the Nightside. Wasn't that long ago I'd been trying to live a normal life in normal London and being spectacularly bad at it. I'd been living in my one-room office, in a building that should have been condemned, sleeping on a cot pushed up against one wall. Eating take-away food and hiding under my desk when the creditors came calling . . . I'd left the Nightside to feel safe. And because I was afraid I was turning into a monster. But there are worse things than that. Failure tastes of cold pizza and over-used tea bags, and the knowledge that you're not really helping anyone, even yourself.

I'll never leave the Nightside again. For all its many sins, it's my home, and I belong there. Along with all the other monsters. And Suzie Shooter, of course. My Suzie.

I got up off the bed, with a certain amount of effort, and went downstairs to see what she was doing. We loved each other as best we could, but I was always the one who had to reach out. Suzie . . . couldn't. But then, I knew that going in. So down the stairs I went, and treading the patterned carpeting was like moving from one world to another. Suzie wasn't what you'd call house-proud.

Her floor looked a lot like her old place—a mess. Dirty and disgusting with overtones of appalling. It was somewhat more hygienic, because I insisted, but the smell always hit me first. Her floor smelled heavy, female, border-line feverish. I peered through the bedroom door in passing. It was empty apart from a pile of blankets in the middle of the floor, churned up like a nest. At least they were clean blankets. Since she wasn't there, I moved on to the living-room, careful to knock on the door first. Suzie didn't react well to surprises.

Suzie was crashed out on her only piece of furniture, a long couch upholstered in deep red leather. *So it won't show the blood,* Suzie had said when I asked, so I stopped asking. She ignored me as I entered the room, her attention fixed on the local news showing on her more modest television set. The room never ceased to depress me. It was bleak, and so empty. Bare wooden floor-boards, bare plaster walls, apart from a huge life-size poster of Diana Rigg as Mrs. Emma Peel in the old *Avengers* TV show. Suzie had scrawled *My Idol* across the bottom, in what looked suspiciously like dried blood.

Her DVDs were stacked in piles against one wall. Her Bruce Lee and Jackie Chan movies, her much-watched copies of *Easy Rider* and Marianne Faithful in *Girl on a Motorcycle.* She also had a fond spot for James Cameron's *Aliens* and his two *Terminator* movies. Plus a whole bunch of Roger Corman's Hells Angels movies, which Suzie always claimed were comedies.

She was wearing her favourite Cleopatra Jones T-shirt over battered blue jeans, and scratching idly at the bare belly between the two, while eating deep-fried calamari nuggets from a bucket. I sat down beside her, and we watched the local news together. The impossibly beautiful presenter was in the middle of a story about a proposed strike by the Nightside sewer workers, who were holding out for bigger flame-throwers and maybe even bazookas. Apparently the giant ants were getting to be a real problem.

Next, a new Timeslip had opened up in a previously un-affected area, and already members of the Really Dangerous Sports Club were racing to the location, so they could throw themselves in and be the first to find out where they'd end up. Nobody was trying to stop them. In the Nightside we're great believers in letting everyone go to Hell in their own way.

And finally, a fanatical Druid terrorist had turned up in the Nightside with his very own backpack nuke wrapped in mistletoe. Fortunately, he had a whole list of demands he wanted to read out first, and he hadn't got half-way through them before Walker turned up, used his commanding Voice on the Druid, and made him eat his bomb, bit by bit. People were already placing bets as to how far he'd get be-fore the plutonium gave him terminal indigestion.

Without looking away from the screen, Suzie reached out and placed her left hand lightly on my thigh. I sat very still, but she took the hand away again almost immedi-ately. She tries hard, but she can't bear to be touched, or to touch anyone else in a friendly way. She was abused as a child, by her own brother; and it left her psychologically scarred. I would have killed the brother, but Suzie beat me to it, years ago. We're working on the problem, taking our time. We're as close as we can be.

So I was surprised when she deliberately put down her calamari bucket, turned to me, and put both her hands on my shoulders. She moved her face in close to mine. I could feel her steady breath on my lips. Her cool, controlled expression didn't change at all, but I could feel the growing tension in her hands on my shoulders, the sheer effort she had to put into such a small gesture. She snatched her hands away and turned her back on me, shaking her head.

"It's all right," I said. Because you have to say something.

"It's not all right! It'll never be all right!" She still wouldn't look at me. "How can I love you when I can't touch you?"

I took her shoulders in my hands, as gently as I could, and turned her back to face me. She tensed under my touch, despite herself. She met my gaze unflinchingly for a moment, then lunged forward, pressing me back against the couch. She put both her hands on my chest and kissed me with painful fierceness. She kissed me for as long as she could stand it, then pushed herself away from me. She jumped up from the couch and moved away from me, hugging herself tightly as though afraid she'd fly apart. I didn't know what to say, or do.

So it was probably just as well that the doorbell rang. I went to answer it, and there at my front door was Walker himself. The man who ran the Nightside, inasmuch as anyone does, or can. A dapper middle-aged gentleman in a smart City suit, complete with old-school tie, bowler hat, and furled umbrella. Anyone else you might have mistaken for someone in the City, some nameless functionary who kept the wheels of business or government turning. But you only had to look into his calm, thoughtful eyes to know how dangerous he was, or could be. Walker had the power of life and death in the Nightside, and it showed. He smiled easily at me.

"Well," I said. "This is . . . unexpected. I didn't think you did house calls. I wasn't even sure you knew where we lived."

"I know where everyone is," said Walker. "All part of the job."

"As a matter of interest," I said, "how did you get past all the mines, man-traps, and shaped charges we put down to discourage the paparazzi?"

"I'm Walker."

"Of course you are. Well, you'd better come in."

"Yes," said Walker.

I took him into Suzie's living-room. He was clearly distressed by the state of the place, but was far too well brought up to say anything. So he smiled brightly, tipped his bowler hat to Suzie, and sat down on the couch without any discernable hesitation. I sat down beside him. Suzie leaned back against the nearest wall, arms tightly folded, glaring unwaveringly at Walker. If he was in any way disturbed, he did a good job of hiding it. Surprisingly, he didn't immediately launch into whatever business had brought him to my home for the very first time. Instead, he made small-talk, was polite and interested and even charming, until I felt like screaming. With Walker, you're always waiting for the other shoe to drop. Usually he speaks to me only when he absolutely has to—when he wants to hire me, or have me killed, or drop me right in it. This new friendly approach . . . just wasn't Walker. But I played along, nodding in all the right places, while Suzie scowled so fiercely it must have hurt her forehead.

Finally, Walker ran out of inconsequential things to say and looked at me thoughtfully. Something big was coming—I could feel it. So I did my best to avert it with other business, if only to assert my independence.

"So," I said. "Did you get all the Parlour's patients safely back to their home dimension?"

"I'm afraid not," said Walker. "Less than half, in the end. Many didn't survive being separated from their life-support technology. Many more died from the shock of what had been done to them. And quite a few were in no fit physical or mental state to be sent anywhere. They're being cared for, in the hope that their condition will improve, but the doctors . . . are not hopeful."

"Less than half?" I said. "I didn't go through all that just to save less than half!"

"You saved as many as you could," said Walker. "That's always been my job—to save as many people as possible."

"Even if you have to sacrifice some of your own people along the way?" I said.

"Exactly," said Walker.

"Why should you get to decide who lives and who dies?" said Suzie.

"I don't," said Walker. "That's up to the Authorities."

"But they're dead," I said. "We were both there when

they were killed and eaten by Lilith's monstrous children. So who . . . exactly . . . pulls your strings these days?"

"The new Authorities," said Walker, smiling pleasantly. "That's why I'm here. I need you to come with me and meet the new Authorities."

I considered him thoughtfully. "Now you know very well I've never got on with authority figures."

"These people . . . are different," said Walker.

"Why now?" I said.

"Because the Walking Man has finally come to the Nightside," said Walker.

I sat up straight, and Suzie pushed herself away from the wall. Walker's voice was as cool and collected as always, but some statements have a power all their own. I would have sworn the room was suddenly colder.

"How do you know it's really him and not just some wannabe?" said Suzie.

"Because it's my business to know things like that," said Walker. "The Walking Man, the wrath of God in the world of men, the most powerful and scariest agent of the Good, ever, has come at last to the Nightside to punish the guilty. And everyone here is either running for the horizon, barricading themselves in while arming themselves to the teeth, or hiding under their beds and wetting themselves. And every single one of them is looking to the new Authorities to do something."

Suzie paced up and down the room, scowling heavily, her thumbs tucked in the top of her jeans. She might have been worried, or she might have been relishing the challenge. She wasn't scared. Suzie didn't get scared or intimidated. Those were things that happened to other people, usually because of Suzie. She sat down abruptly on the edge of the couch, next to me. Close though she was, she still didn't quite touch me. I caught Walker noticing that, and he nodded slowly.

"So close," he said. "In every way but one."

I gave him my best hard look, but to his credit he didn't flinch. "Is there anything you don't know about?" I said.

He smiled briefly. "You'd be surprised."

"It's none of your business," said Suzie. "And if you say anything to anyone, I'll kill you."

"You'd be surprised how many people already know, or guess," said Walker. "It's hard to keep secrets in the Nightside. I am merely . . . concerned."

"Why?" I said bluntly. "What are we, to you? What have I ever been to you, except a threat to your precious status quo, or an expendable agent for some mission too dangerous or too dirty for your own people? And now, suddenly, you're *concerned* about me? Why, for God's sake?"

"Because you're my son," said Walker. "In every way that matters."

He couldn't have surprised me more if he'd taken out a gun and shot me. Suzie and I looked blankly at each other, then back at Walker, but he gave every indication of being perfectly serious. He smiled briefly, holding his dignity close about him.

"We've never really talked, have we?" he said. "Only shared a few threats and insults, in passing . . . or discussed the details of some case we had to work on together. All very brisk and businesslike. You can't afford to get too close to someone you know you may have to kill one day. But things are different now, in so many ways."

"I thought you had two sons?" I said. I didn't know what else to say.

"Oh yes," said Walker. "Good boys, both of them. We don't talk. What could we talk about? I've gone to great pains to ensure that neither they nor their mother has any idea what it is I do for a living. They know nothing about the Nightside, or the terrible things I have to do here, just to keep the peace. I couldn't bear it if they knew. They might look at me as though I were some kind of monster. I used to be so good at keeping my two lives separate. Two lives, two Walkers, doing my best to give equal time to both. But the Nightside is a jealous mistress . . . and what used to be my real life, my sane and rational life, got sacrificed to the greater good.

"My boys, my fine boys . . . are strangers to me now. You're all I've got, John. The only son of my oldest friend. I'd forgotten how much that time meant to me, until I met your father again during the Lilith War. Those happy days of our youth . . . We thought we were going to change the world; and unfortunately we did. Now your father is gone, again, and you're all I've got left, John. Perhaps the nearest thing to a real son I'll ever have. The only son who could ever hope to understand me."

"How many times have you tried to kill me?" I said. "Directly, or indirectly?"

"That's family for you," said Walker. "In the Night-side."

I looked at him for a long time.

"Don't listen to him," said Suzie. "You can't believe him. It's Walker."

"The words *manipulative* and *emotional blackmail* do spring to mind," I said. "This is all so sudden, Walker."

"I know," he said calmly. "I put it all down to midlife crisis myself."

"And where does all this leave us?" I said.

"Exactly where we were before," said Walker. "We'll still probably end up having to kill each other, someday. For what will no doubt seem like perfectly good reasons at the time. But it means . . . I'm allowed to be concerned. About you, and Suzie. And no, you don't get a say in the matter."

"We're doing fine," said Suzie. "We're making progress."

She let one arm rest casually across my shoulders. And I hope only I could tell what the effort cost her.

"Let us talk about the Walking Man," I said. Everything else could wait till later, after I'd had more time to think about it. "He's never come here before. So, why now?"

"In the past, the Nightside's unique nature kept out all direct agents of Heaven and Hell," said Walker. "But since Lilith was banished again, it appears a subtle change has come over the Nightside, and many things that were not possible before are cropping up now with regrettable reg-ularity."

"So all kinds of agents for the Good could be turning up here?" I said.

"Or agents of Evil," said Suzie.

"Well, quite," murmured Walker. "As if things weren't complicated enough . . ."

"Still," I said, "what's bringing the Walking Man here *now*?"

"It would appear he disapproves of the new Authorities," said Walker. "The group whose interests I now represent."

"That's why you're here!" I said. "Because if they're in danger, so are you!"

Walker smiled and said nothing.

"Who are they?" said Suzie. "These new Authorities? The old bunch were nothing more than faceless businessmen who ran things because they owned most of the Nightside. So, are we talking about their families? The next generation? Meet the new boss, same as the old boss, don't get screwed again?"

"The inheritors?" said Walker, with something very like a sniff. "They wish. We saw them off. One quick glimpse of what actually goes on here, and they couldn't sell their holdings fast enough. No . . . Certain personages in the Nightside have come together to represent the main interests in this place. Essentially, the Nightside is now determined to run itself."

"Who, exactly?" I said. "Who are these brand-new *self-appointed* Authorities? Do I know them?"

"Some of them, certainly," said Walker. "They all know you. That's why I'm here."

"How can you serve people from the Nightside?" I said, honestly curious. "You've never made any secret about your feelings for us. You always said the best thing to do would be to nuke the place and wipe out the whole damned freak show once and for all."

"I've mellowed," said Walker. "Just possibly, these new Authorities can bring about real change, from within. I would like to see that, before I die. Now, come with me and meet the new Authorities. Hear what they have to say; learn what they mean to do. Before the Walking Man tracks them down and kills them all."

"But what do they want with me and Suzie?" I said.

Walker raised an eyebrow. "I would have thought that was obvious. They want you to use your gift to find the Walking Man, then find a way to stop him. Shall we go?"

AVAILABLE NOW IN HARDCOVER FROM
*NEW YORK TIMES* BESTSELLING AUTHOR
# Simon R. Green

# JUST ANOTHER JUDGEMENT DAY
## A NOVEL OF THE NIGHTSIDE

*Come to the Nightside, where the clocks always read three A.M., where terrible things happen with predictable regularity, and where the always-dark streets are full of people partying like Judgement Day will never come.*

Judgement Day has arrived and the Walking Man, God's own enforcer whose sole purpose in life is to eliminate the wicked and the guilty, has come to the Nightside. Given the nature of the Nightside, there's a good chance that once he gets started, he'll just keep on going until there's no-one left. Private investigator John Taylor has been hired by the Authorities to stop him. But legend has it that he can't be killed...

**"A macabre and thoroughly entertaining world."**
**—Jim Butcher,**
**author of the Dresden Files series**

penguin.com